Pra
the Blu

"As soon as I finis... wait to start the next one. No books have ever made me do that before."
— *Terrance W.*

"The suspense got to be so great I could feel the blood pounding in my ears."
— *Yolanda E.*

"Once I started reading them, I just couldn't stop, not even to go to sleep."
— *Brian M.*

"These books are SO REAL. What you see in these books really happens. That's why you can't stop reading."
— *Phillip C.*

"The last thing I wanted to do was read a Bluford book or any book. But after a few pages, I couldn't put the book down. I felt like I was a witness in the story, like I was inside it."
— *Ray F.*

"I found it very easy to lose myself in these books. They kept my interest from beginning to end and were always realistic. The characters are vivid, and the endings left me in eager anticipation of the next book."
— *Keziah J.*

"I like the Bluford Series because it's action-packed all the way through."
—*Adam F.*

"My school is just like Bluford High. The characters are just like people I know. These books are real!"
—*Jessica K.*

"I thought the Bluford Series was going to be boring, but once I started, I couldn't stop reading. I had to keep going just to see what would happen next. I have to admit I enjoyed myself. Now I'm done, and I can't wait for more books."
—*Jamal C.*

"When I finished these books, I went back to the beginning and read them all over again. That's how much I loved them."
— *Caren B.*

"I've been reading these books for the last three days and can't get them out of my mind. They are that good!"
—*Stephen B.*

"I have never been so interested in any type of book in my entire life. I'm just surprised to see how much they catch my attention. Once I started reading, I could not stop. I was up all the way into the midnight hours trying to finish. The Bluford books didn't bore me or make me feel like I was wasting my time. I'm so glad I found them."
—*Desiree G.*

Blood Is Thicker

Paul Langan and D.M. Blackwell

Series Editor: Paul Langan

TOWNSEND PRESS

Books in the Bluford Series

Copyright © 2004 by Townsend Press, Inc.
Printed in the United States of America

20 19 18 17 16 15 14 13 12 11

Cover illustration © 2004 by Gerald Purnell

cs@townsendpress.com

ISBN-13: 978-1-59194-016-6
ISBN-10: 1-59194-016-8

Library of Congress Control Number:
2003110888

Chapter 1

"Goodbye, Darcy," Hakeem Randall said, gently letting go of Darcy Wills, his girlfriend for the past year. The tears in her eyes were like daggers slicing deep into his heart.

"Goodbye, Hakeem."

He watched her walk down the short driveway. If there was anything he could do to stop his family from moving away, he would have done it. But the decision was out of his hands.

Squinting under the Monday morning sun, Hakeem felt like someone had wrapped him in a heavy blanket of gloom. He wouldn't see Darcy again this summer. Maybe not ever. And in just a matter of hours, his old friends at Bluford High School and his home in southern California would be thousands of miles away.

"I'm gonna miss you, girl," he mumbled as Darcy turned the corner and disappeared. "You and everything else."

Just weeks ago, his parents had informed him that they were moving the family to Detroit to live with Uncle James and Aunt Lorraine. The news struck Hakeem like a bomb blast, turning his world upside down overnight. Yet, as bad as it was, the announcement wasn't the worst thing he heard recently.

Five months ago, his father was diagnosed with kidney cancer. Surgery, chemotherapy, and the sickness it caused had reduced Dad's strength so much that he could no longer perform his job as a warehouse manager. For three months, Hakeem watched as his father's size diminished and his face aged. Though the treatment had stopped the disease, it left Dad a shadow of his former self, and it devastated the family's savings.

"We've spent everything we had on medical bills, baby," Mom said tearfully a few weeks ago. "I don't know what's gonna happen. But no matter what, I need you to be strong, Hakeem. I need you to be the man around here."

Hakeem nodded solemnly in response, expecting that the family would find a small apartment nearby. He was even ready to share a bedroom with his seven-year-old twin sisters so his parents could save money. But Hakeem never imagined that his Uncle James would invite the family to Detroit or that Dad would agree to go.

"I don't know what choice we have," Hakeem's father explained when he told the family the news. "Even though the cancer's stopped, the doctors say it could be months before I get my strength back. And without our savings, we can't afford to stay here any more," he said, massaging his forehead, his scratchy voice sounding much older than his forty years. "I wish I didn't have to do this to you. I'm sorry."

"Don't worry, Dad. It'll be all right," Hakeem had replied, half believing his words. Besides their money problems, Hakeem knew there was always a chance the cancer could return, a possibility which kept him up many nights, his heart racing with fear. In a few days, Dad would meet with doctors in Detroit to see if the cancer was still in remission.

Even though no one admitted it, Hakeem knew one reason Dad was moving them to Detroit was to keep his family together in case his health took a turn for the worse.

Watching the movers load his family's belongings into the storage truck, Hakeem felt as he had years earlier when someone robbed his church. The stolen money had been collected for a little girl who had leukemia, but that didn't stop the thieves from taking every cent. He had decided then that life was cruel. His father's cancer diagnosis, his horrific battle with the disease, and the sudden move were just the latest proof.

"You all right, Hakeem?" Dad asked, snapping Hakeem from his thoughts. "I know it isn't easy sayin' goodbye to your friends, especially Darcy."

"I'm fine, Dad. Darcy and I said what we had to say," Hakeem replied, trying to hide his sadness. *Be strong*, he reminded himself.

"That's it," his mother said as the movers closed the back of the truck. "Everything's packed, and the airport taxi is here. We gotta leave now. Come on, everyone."

Hakeem grabbed his suitcase, the

notebook he used as a journal, and his old guitar, and took one last look at his house. Without furniture and pictures, it was a cold and empty shell, not the place where he grew up.

I can't believe I'm not coming back, he thought, glancing down the street toward his school, Bluford High, just a few blocks away.

I need you to be the man around here, his mother's words echoed in his mind.

"Come on, son," his father urged. The family was waiting in the cab.

Hakeem took a deep breath, wiped his eyes, and said a silent goodbye to his world.

Good men beat down
Smiles turn to frowns
There is no logic
In a world so tragic

Hakeem read the words from his notebook. He had written them when his father first mentioned the move to Detroit. It seemed as if years had passed, not weeks. He flipped the page bitterly.

The dull hum of the plane's engines had lulled the rest of his family to sleep, but Hakeem could not relax. His mind swirled with thoughts of Darcy and his closest friends, Cooper and Tarah.

Maybe one day he'd write a song for them, he thought. Hakeem turned to a blank sheet of paper and stared at the tiny blue lines on the page. For years, he'd been singing and playing his guitar. He joined his church choir in second grade. Later, when he developed a stuttering problem in middle school, he discovered that it disappeared whenever he sang. Years ago, Mr. Smalley, the choir director, praised his voice.

"God gave you some talents, young man. Be sure you use them."

Hakeem hadn't sung for the church in years. But he did perform from time to time at Bluford. Even when he wasn't singing, he was always jotting lyrics in his notebook for songs he might sing one day. Music and writing were two things he relied on when the rest of the world was a mess. In his songs, he could control everything. There was no cancer. No goodbyes. Not unless he decided it.

Hakeem glanced at the notebook and tried to remember everything he knew about Detroit. He'd been there once before. It was ten years ago, when he was just six years old. Then, his father was to him the strongest person in the world. A person immune to disease, to cancer and chemotherapy. A superhero.

What Hakeem did most during the visit was eat huge dinners at his aunt and uncle's house and play video games with his cousin Savon. The two boys were nearly the same age, though Savon was much heavier.

"Savon's a husky boy," his mother used to say.

During the weeks he stayed in Detroit, Hakeem and Savon played for hours on end. Hakeem remembered once the two were playing catch in the street when some teens stole their ball.

"Thanks, Wimpy and Blimpy," the teens mocked as they strolled down the street, passing the ball around. The moment had stuck in Hakeem's mind. The teasing hurt, but it had also made him feel close to his cousin. They shared a special bond that moment. They were family.

But when Hakeem returned to California, he gradually lost touch with Savon. An awkward phone conversation three years ago at Christmas was the last time they talked. And now, after so many years, the dim memory of Detroit was bittersweet, a reminder of a past long gone.

Staring out of the small window next to his seat, Hakeem watched a veil of wispy clouds pass beneath him. His memories did little to erase the hole the move was carving into his life.

I miss home already, he thought, stretching back in his seat and closing his eyes.

I miss home.

"Are we there yet? Are we at Uncle James's house?" asked Charlene, one of Hakeem's younger twin sisters.

"Almost," Dad said wearily from the passenger seat of the rental car. Since Dad got sick, Mom drove the family everywhere.

"You've been asking that ever since we landed," snapped Charmaine, rolling her eyes at her sister. "Can't you just stop talking?"

Hakeem yawned and said nothing. The hour wait to get off the plane and pick up their bags was tiring. Now, the twenty-five minute drive through city traffic to Uncle James's house felt like slow torture. His sisters only made it worse.

"Is this it?" Charlene asked suddenly as the car stopped at a traffic light. "Is this where we're going to live at?"

"Shut up," Charmaine groaned.

"Girls!" Mom snapped. "If you don't stop whining, I'm gonna give you both somethin' to whine about."

"Make a right up there on Sawyer Street," Dad interrupted. His tired voice silenced everyone.

Outside, the houses were older and more densely packed than those back home. Made of red brick, many were row homes, though a few bigger houses did stand alone on some blocks. At the end of one street, Hakeem spotted a playground with a swing set and basketball court. A steel fence surrounded the park, making it look more like a prison yard than a playground.

Several teenage boys were shooting baskets as Hakeem and his family passed. One reminded Hakeem of his best friend, Cooper Hodden. Coop was one of the toughest people he knew, but he was also one of the nicest. When he found out that Hakeem was moving away, Coop had almost cried.

"Stay with *us*, Hak! My mom says we

9

got room for you," he insisted. "Besides, she likes you more than she likes me."

For a second, Hakeem had considered Cooper's offer. He desperately wanted to stay, but he couldn't abandon his family. Not with everyone depending on him. Still, as he gazed out at the unfamiliar neighborhood, part of him wished he'd listened to Coop.

On a corner up ahead, Hakeem noticed two guys sitting on the steps of a house. One had a sharp angular face and wore a sideways baseball cap. The other was shaved bald and shirtless, his chest as wide as a barrel. Both glared at the car as the family approached.

Hakeem felt a nervous twinge in the pit of his stomach. Seeming to sense tension, Hakeem's mother pushed the accelerator, and the rented sedan lurched forward.

Welcome to the neighborhood, Hakeem thought bitterly to himself.

As they drove further up Sawyer Street, the homes gradually began to resemble what Hakeem remembered from his childhood. Some featured small porches with chairs and iron railings. Others had driveways and tiny front yards lined with flowers. While an occasional house was boarded up and empty, most looked recently painted.

"One more block," Dad said, as the car passed two young boys racing each other along the sidewalk. Hakeem remembered how he and Savon had run up and down the streets years earlier. He wondered what his cousin would be like today.

Mom slowed the car to a stop in front of a green and white three-story house. "Here we are," she announced, her voice more relieved than excited.

"It's smaller than I remember it," Hakeem said.

"That's because you're bigger," Dad replied with a haggard smile. Though his face looked older, his intense black eyes were as clear as ever. "Looks like James had the house painted. The color's different," he added.

"How did you remember something like that?" Mom asked, unbuckling her seatbelt.

"My memory still works even if the rest of me ain't what it used to be. That house used to be bright yellow, kind of an eyesore. Good thing they repainted it." Dad chuckled then, a sound as scratchy and dry as sandpaper.

Hakeem cringed at Dad's raspy laughter, a scar of the illness that had threatened his father and driven them out of their home. Keeping his thoughts to himself, he stepped out onto the curb and scanned his new neighborhood.

At the end of the block, a fire hydrant gushed water into the street. In front of it, a crowd of children splashed loudly, their joyful screeches mocking Hakeem's mood. Somewhere far off, sirens screamed into the summer air, while overhead, a jet plane rumbled across the sky. Across the street, a mottled German shepherd growled menacingly from a nearby porch.

Hakeem shook his head at the strange chorus of sounds. He felt as if he'd just been dropped into the center of a strange and hostile world.

"They're here!" a husky voice called out from behind an open window. "It's about time."

Hakeem glanced up from the trunk and saw a muscular young man with tightly braided cornrows step out of the house and come toward his mother. He wore a white T-shirt and navy blue and white striped athletic pants. A thick silvery chain with a glimmering letter S

12

hung from his neck. Hakeem didn't recognize him.

"Savon? Is that you?" Hakeem's mother asked.

Savon? Hakeem's jaw dropped. It couldn't be. The person who stood before them looked nothing like the overweight kid from years earlier. Instead, he resembled a middleweight boxer.

"Who else would I be?" Savon asked, strutting down the short walkway with his thick arms swaying from side to side. "Wassup, Uncle Henry," Savon said, as he approached the car. "How you doin', Aunt Selma?"

Hakeem's mother threw her arms around Savon. "I can't believe my eyes, Savon. My Lord, I almost didn't even recognize you. You've grown into quite a young man."

"Well, that's what happens when you don't see somebody for ten years," Savon said proudly. "Last time you saw me I was just a chubby kid," he added.

"Ten years is too long for a family not to see each other," Hakeem's mother replied, shaking her head at her own comment. "Where does the time go? You kids grow up so fast."

"Aw, don't start gettin' sentimental on me, Auntie. Looks like we're gonna have lotsa time now," he added and then turned to Hakeem. "What up, cuz?" Savon asked, his eyes squinting slightly. "Now *you* don't look that different from back in the day. Maybe a little taller, that's all."

Hakeem could easily see over Savon's head. He had to be at least two inches taller than his cousin. But Savon was definitely more muscular—and probably stronger. Yet what struck Hakeem most about Savon was his eyes. They seemed almost angry. "Man, you always were skinny, cuz. But now you look like a toothpick," Savon added. Even his voice seemed to have a bitter edge.

Hakeem blinked for a second, unsure how to respond. Was his cousin kidding, or was he trying to start trouble?

"That's all right, Savon. I remember you being a little thick in the middle. Looks like some of that thickness left your stomach and went to your head," Hakeem replied playfully, trying to turn the moment into a joke. He then offered his hand to shake Savon's.

"I guess we can't all be as perfect as

14

you, huh, *cuz*?" Savon said. There was an icy bite to his voice, and he ignored Hakeem's outstretched hand. "But it's all good 'cause while you spent years bein' everybody's favorite son, I spent some time hittin' the weights. And from what I see, weights would do your skinny butt some good," he snapped.

Hakeem swallowed hard. He was stunned, but no one seemed to hear the comment his cousin made. For an instant, he felt his old stutter beginning to seize him. Though the problem was nearly cured, it flared up when he was stressed or nervous. He shook his head and tried to think of a comeback.

Just then, his little sisters sprinted up to him, grabbing his arm.

"Mom said for you to unload the trunk," Charmaine said nervously.

Savon looked down at them then and laughed. "Oh no, you brought rugrats!" he exclaimed. "Two of them!"

"We ain't no rats," Charlene protested, "so don't be callin' us that."

"Don't get mad, I was just teasin' you," Savon said. "You better get used to that 'cause I do a lot of it."

Charlene frowned and moved closer to Hakeem, as if she was looking for protection. He put his hand on her shoulder.

"It's okay, Charlene. He's just playin', that's all—"

"Oh, thank God you made it!" a woman's voice interrupted. "I been prayin' ever since you left California!"

Hakeem turned to see his Aunt Lorraine standing on the porch. She looked heavier than he remembered, but she still had a sweet, round face and a warm, inviting smile.

"And look at the toothpick they brought with 'em," Savon laughed, pointing his finger at Hakeem. "Hakeem's as skinny as he was when we were kids," he added.

Hakeem seethed at the comment but smiled out of respect for his aunt.

"Oh, he's just fine," Aunt Lorraine said, waving Savon away with her hand. "And he's good-looking, too. I bet you had all the girls back home chasin' after you."

Hakeem blushed and shook his head as she came closer to him. "I do okay," he said, thinking of Darcy and their painful breakup.

Savon seemed to be annoyed at his mother's comment. He frowned and stepped away while she approached.

"I missed you, Aunt Lorraine," Hakeem said, giving her a hug.

"I missed you too, baby. It has been too long. Way too long. I keep telling myself that all this trouble is a blessing in disguise. It's a way for all of us to get to know each other again." Letting him go, she turned her attention to Hakeem's sisters. "And look at you two!" she cheered, wrapping them both in a massive embrace. "I am so happy to finally see you!"

Hakeem smiled, nearly forgetting the painful events that had forced them to Detroit.

"C'mon, Cali-boy." Savon's rough voice jarred him like an alarm clock. "We got work to do."

17

Chapter 2

"Let's get your stuff inside," Savon said, leading Hakeem to the trunk of the rental car. The rest of the family went into the house, leaving them alone.

"This all you got?" Savon asked, peering into the trunk and eyeing the suitcases.

"We put our stuff in storage," Hakeem said, refusing to admit to his cousin that his parents could not afford to ship all their belongings to Detroit.

Savon grunted and then hoisted the heaviest suitcase out of the trunk as if it were weightless. Then, he reached for Hakeem's guitar case.

"It's okay, Savon. I'll take that," Hakeem said. Savon looked at him curiously for an instant.

"You're sharin' my room, cuz," Savon said with a smirk. "Whatever is yours has to go up to the third floor. You sure you can handle it? You lookin' a little broke-down."

Hakeem rolled his eyes. Savon's comment was bad enough. But the news that he'd have to share a bedroom with him was even worse. "Man, don't worry about me," Hakeem grumbled, grabbing his guitar and following his cousin.

Hakeem was tired when he and Savon finished unloading the car. The trip up three flights of steps made his face wet with perspiration and his arms burn. He tried his best to hide his exhaustion, taking deep breaths when his cousin was not looking. Afterwards, they sat on the front porch drinking orange soda. Hakeem remembered it was Savon's favorite drink when they were kids.

"You ain't worn out from that little bit of liftin', are you?" Savon asked with a superior grin. "I mean, I feel like we was just gettin' started. I was 'bout ready to go bench press a couple hundred pounds," he bragged. "You wanna lift with me?"

"Man, you didn't get up at 6:00 a.m.,

19

fly halfway across the country, and leave all your friends behind. I'm tired," Hakeem admitted.

"Don't tell me you're asking me to feel sorry for you. You don't even want to go there, not with me. You think I wanna be sharin' my room with you? *Please!*" Savon scoffed. He looked genuinely disgusted. Again, Hakeem was caught off guard.

"Savon, what's your prob—"

"Check it out, yo. There go my homeboys," Savon interjected, jumping out of his chair and rushing off the porch.

Hakeem watched as his cousin approached a group of guys gathered in the street. Including Savon, there were five of them. One had a Rottweiler which he restrained with a thick leash. The dog seemed friendly, but it looked as if it could devour a small child if it wanted to.

"Wassup, partnas?" Savon called out as he crossed the street.

"'Sup, Savon," answered one of the guys, as he blew a whitish-gray cloud of cigarette smoke into the air.

"We just wanted to know if you was still down wit' Friday night?" another guy asked.

"You know I'm down, Tariq," Savon

asserted. "You think I'm gettin' soft or somethin'?"

"We was just checkin'," the kid answered. "Ain't nothin' to get hyped about."

"Oh, you ain't seen me get hyped!" Savon exclaimed. "Just wait 'til Friday night!"

The guys laughed. "I just hope we get out 'fore the cops come," said Tariq, glancing for a second at Hakeem.

"Man, they ain't nothin' to worry about."

Hakeem nearly dropped his soda. Right in front of him, Savon was boasting about something illegal and dangerous. Hakeem tried to listen to the conversation, but a passing truck momentarily masked Savon's voice.

Even with the noise, Hakeem could see that his cousin dominated the conversation. Savon was a blur of motion, wildly moving his arms and occasionally punching his fist into the air to emphasize a point. Savon's friends laughed and nodded at what he was saying.

"Savon, Hakeem, come inside," Aunt Lorraine called from inside the house.

"Yo, I'll catch up wit' y'all later on," Savon said to the group of guys as he headed toward the house.

"You know where to find us," one of the guys called out.

Savon returned to porch and glared at Hakeem. "What was you doin', listenin' to every word?"

"No, I—"

"That's what I thought," Savon snapped. "You didn't hear *nothin'*!"

Aunt Lorraine ushered the family into the modest dining room, where a full spread of food was waiting. There were fried chicken, macaroni and cheese, homemade corn bread, and a pineapple upside down cake. The aroma reminded Hakeem of his visit years earlier. Back then Aunt Lorraine put homemade dishes on the table almost every night. She cooked so much good food that Hakeem's dad called her "the magician in the kitchen."

"Everybody dig in," she said, after saying a brief prayer. Then she smiled and heaped a huge spoonful of macaroni onto Hakeem's plate. "Now I want you all to make yourselves at home. This is how we eat around here. Which is probably why I can't seem to lose any of this weight," she chuckled.

"Are we always gonna have this much food?" Charlene asked.

"At least until September, baby," Aunt Lorraine answered, putting a chicken leg on her plate. "One good thing about bein' a third-grade teacher is that I get my summers off, and when I'm home, I like to cook up a storm, especially when we got guests." Lorraine smiled as she talked.

"So, where's James?" Hakeem's father asked. "How come he's not eating with us?"

"He ain't ever here," Savon said, reaching an arm in front of Hakeem to get a piece of chicken.

"Oh, he's working," Aunt Lorraine explained. "I ain't never known a man that works the way he does. He's at that furniture store practically from morning 'til night, seven days a week."

"His brother used to be the same way," Hakeem's mother said, putting her hand on Dad's arm. "He was at that job so much I used to call it his 'second home.' We hardly ever saw him with the hours he kept."

"That's just the way we were brought up. Our dad was from the South, and he told us that the only way a black man can make it in the world was to work harder and smarter than the next guy. So that's what we did."

"Yeah, well, some kids today don't seem to know a thing about that lesson," said Aunt Lorraine, glancing at Savon.

For an instant, a tense silence swept over the table. Hakeem took a sip of his drink, and Savon grabbed a piece of cornbread. Hakeem's sisters looked at their parents.

"James is working late tonight because there was a break-in near the store a few nights ago," Aunt Lorraine said.

"A break-in!" Mom exclaimed. "That's terrible."

"Mmm hmmm," Aunt Lorraine nodded, swallowing a mouthful of macaroni. "Two stores been robbed on the street in the past month."

"I told him to get a guard dog," Savon said. "A pit bull or a rottie. That'd keep them thieves away. If he'd just—"

"Hush your mouth, boy," Aunt Lorraine snapped. "You always talkin' nonsense. He don't need no guard dog down there, but what he could use right now is some extra help." Aunt Lorraine glared at Savon as she spoke.

"Mom, I told you. I ain't got time for the store right now," Savon said.

"But you got time for them friends of yours, right?"

Savon slouched back in his chair for a second and crossed his arms.

"Well, Hakeem and I are glad to pitch in," Dad suggested, breaking the tension. "Looks like we got plenty of time now."

"It's the least we can do," Dad continued, looking at Hakeem. "As soon as I get my strength back, I'd love to help James out. Lord knows I could use the exercise. But Hakeem could pitch in right away. Maybe tomorrow if James needed him, right, Hakeem?"

Hakeem felt the eyes of everyone at the table focus on him. He'd never thought about working with his uncle, but now he realized he had no choice.

"Yeah, sure," Hakeem said, shrugging his shoulders. "I'll help out."

Suddenly, Savon turned to Hakeem's father and stood up. "Yo, do you all mind if I excuse myself?" he asked. "I got some calls to make, and I want to get the room ready for Mr. Cali over here."

"But Savon," Aunt Lorraine protested, "we have guests—"

"It's all right, Lorraine," Dad said. "Let him do what he's gotta do. Savon'll be seeing a lot of us."

Savon was already on his way up the stairs by the time Dad finished talking. Aunt Lorraine shook her head as the thud of Savon sprinting up the steps faded in the distance.

"You'll have to ignore your nephew, Henry. Most times his mouth works faster than his mind does."

"It's all right," Dad replied. "I was sixteen once. That's just part of the territory."

"But I really worry about him, Henry," Aunt Lorraine said. "I wish he had his act together like you, Hakeem." She reached over and patted Hakeem's forearm as she spoke. "We keep tellin' Savon about how well you've done in school and how you help out the family, but he just doesn't want to listen these days."

Hakeem smiled blankly, hiding his growing discomfort. During the rest of the meal, he listened as the adults talked. But his mind kept drifting back to Savon and the mysterious conversation that happened outside.

What were they planning for Friday night? he wondered.

If it was anything like it sounded, Aunt Lorraine had good reason to worry.

"This is *my* room," barked Savon as soon as Hakeem walked into the small bedroom, "and you're just a *guest.* So, remember not to mess wit' any of my stuff."

Hakeem nodded and walked to the far corner of the room, where his belongings were piled. Savon was stretched out on his bed leafing through a wrinkled magazine. He flipped through rapidly, skipping pages that did not contain pictures.

How am I gonna live here with him? Hakeem thought to himself as he looked around.

The floor of the small bedroom was cluttered with sneakers, piles of clothing, and stacks of CD's. A small desk with a clip-on lamp sat in one corner of the room next to Savon's bed. An empty Coke bottle, a stereo, a tiny cactus, and a pile of magazines took up nearly all of the desk space. A full-length mirror was attached to the back of the bedroom door, and posters of hip-hop artists covered most of the walls. One even covered the closet door. The posters reminded

Hakeem of the music store at the mall back home. The store was so loud and crowded that it usually gave him a headache.

The only thing Hakeem was happy to see was a window located at the foot of Savon's bed. The window was open, and a breeze cut some of the heat that filled the room. A second single bed with a black metal frame and a bowed mattress lined the far wall. Diagonally across from it was a chest of drawers and a lamp. Hakeem figured the empty bed was his. Without a word, he piled his stuff on the mattress, sat down, and took a deep breath.

Somehow the cramped room made him feel even further from home. A heavy wave of sadness spread over him. *If only I could have stayed at Coop's*, Hakeem thought to himself.

"What's the matter?" Savon asked, interrupting his thoughts. "You expectin' a palace or somethin'? This ain't good enough for you? No sunshine? No beaches?"

"Savon, you need to chill," Hakeem said, raising his voice.

"Don't tell me what I need to do," Savon hissed. "I don't need to hear that from nobody, especially you. You don't know nothin' about me or what I need."

Hakeem glared at Savon. His pulse suddenly began to throb in his neck.

"Savon, what's your p-p-problem?!" Hakeem snapped, his stutter surfacing uncontrollably. "I haven't done anything to you, and all I get from you is s-s-sta-tic."

"You've got to be kidding me," Savon said, his jaw dropping. "Is that a stutter I hear? I guess you ain't so perfect after all."

Hakeem squeezed his hands into fists and took a deep breath. He knew the only way to stop the stutter was to relax.

"Uh-oh. Are you getting mad too?" Savon challenged, putting his magazine down. "You oughta be careful. This ain't California."

"Man, what's your problem? You keep acting like I did something to you when you know I didn't. Besides, we're family. We ain't supposed to be this way."

Savon winced for an instant, as if the words stung. "Oh, so now you're trying to tell me how I'm supposed to be too? I don't need no advice, cuz. Not from you,

Dad, or anyone. And what you need is a speech doctor. I gotta bounce," Savon muttered bitterly, tossing aside his magazine.

Before Hakeem could reply, Savon rose from his bed, grabbed a baseball cap, and walked out. "Leave my stuff alone," he barked as he descended the steps.

The room was suddenly quiet. Hakeem leaned back on the crooked mattress and stared at the ceiling. He had never missed home more.

Out here, in strange places,
nowhere to hide,
don't know where my space is.

Out there, you walk alone
miles between us
I can't come home.

Some day, who knows when,
if fates allow
we'll meet again.

Hakeem penned the words into his journal and read them. They were for his friends and the home he left behind. But most of all, they were for Darcy. As he read, he imagined how she'd react to

30

Savon.

"Why are you acting like some hard-core gangster?" she would say. *"Muscles and jewelry don't make you better than anyone else."* The image of her scolding Savon made Hakeem smile, but it also made him homesick.

Savon had been gone for more than an hour, and in that time, Hakeem had finished unpacking his few things. After sitting briefly with his family, he grabbed his guitar and journal and sat on the back step as the daylight faded away.

Back home, he would watch sunsets with Darcy and their friends. They would laugh and talk about their fears and plans for the future, but never in all those evenings did his fears include Dad's cancer or moving away. Never did he picture that he'd end up in Detroit with his angry cousin.

Hakeem closed his journal and gently picked up his guitar. The sky was almost completely black, and a cool breeze drifted through his uncle's small backyard. The guitar's neck was smooth and familiar in Hakeem's hand.

He played a sad melody that matched his mood. The music comforted him, making him feel as if he had a close friend next to him, one that understood everything he was experiencing. Losing himself, Hakeem leaned into the guitar as he played, making it speak his mind, vent his anger, voice his frustration. His fingers ached when he finally stopped playing, but he felt relieved.

Then he heard someone clapping.

In the yard next door, Hakeem spotted a young woman watching him. For an instant, he was frozen.

"Hi," she said, smiling warmly. "Don't stop playing. It's really nice."

Hakeem blushed. He had not been playing a song. He'd played his private feelings. Knowing that she had been watching him made him suddenly feel naked. He tried to think of a song to play, but his mind went blank.

"I didn't realize I had an audience," he said, taking his fingers off the strings. "How long have you been . . . watching me?"

"Just a few minutes. I was really enjoying the show."

"*Show*?" Hakeem said, watching her closely. She was leaning against the metal fence that separated the two backyards. In the glow of a nearby street light, Hakeem could see that she was stunning, perhaps his age or a bit older. Her dark skin was flawless, and her hair was cut short, making her look like a model from a fashion magazine. "If I knew there was a crowd, I would have sold tickets," he joked.

She smiled again, and her face seemed to glow. Hakeem's heart fluttered. "I'm sorry I snuck up on you, but I'm not used to hearing a guitar playing out here, so I had to investigate. It's not everyday a girl gets a live performance in her backyard. I didn't mean to ruin your vibe."

"That's okay," Hakeem replied, putting the guitar down. "I was just messing around, nothing serious."

"Well, it sure sounded serious to me. To be honest with you, I never heard a guitar sound so . . . pretty."

"Thanks," Hakeem said, unsure whether he liked her description of his music. "I play when I need to clear my head. It helps me relax, you know?"

"I wish I could play like that," she said. "Whenever I need to get away, I listen to music. I don't make my own." For an instant, Hakeem thought he heard a sad note in her voice.

"Maybe you could take guitar lessons," Hakeem suggested. "You better watch out, though. People may start spying on you when you least expect it," he added, smiling.

"Maybe you could teach me?" she replied, seeming to ignore his comment. Hakeem could see a playful glint in her eye.

"That's a lot to ask someone you don't even know."

"You're right," she said, walking over to the fence directly across from him. "That's why you should introduce yourself to me. What's your name?"

Hakeem blinked, unprepared for her question. "I'm Hakeem," he said.

"Well, it's nice to meet you, Hakeem. I'm Anika," she said, moving closer and wrapping her fingers into the wire fence. "So tell me, what are you doing in my neighbor's backyard?"

"This is my aunt and uncle's house. My family and I just moved in from California."

"Oh, *you're* that cousin Savon's been talkin' about?"

"You talk to Savon?" Hakeem asked.

"Not so much anymore, but I hear him all the time," Anika replied, crossing her arms. "He's always hangin' on the corner with his crew, and you can't miss his big mouth when he's talkin'. I heard him complainin' the other day 'bout how he had to share his room with some cousin from 'Cali.'" As she spoke, Anika mimicked Savon's voice and manner.

Hakeem smiled at her imitation. "No wonder I got such a warm welcome," he said.

"Well, if you ask me, it was *you* who got the bad end of that deal, not him." Anika tilted her head and raised her eyebrow to emphasize her point.

Hakeem rubbed his chin and tried to hide how much he enjoyed Anika's company. She was so pretty, and she seemed completely honest. Looking at her, he couldn't help noticing her body, the way her hips filled her denim skirt, the way her stomach was visible just beneath her snug T-shirt.

"So, you and Savon have known each other for a long time?" Hakeem asked.

"Ever since fifth grade, though it feels like forever. That's when my mom skipped town with her smooth-talkin' boyfriend," Anika said bitterly. "She sent me here to stay with my grandma, and I been here ever since. But all that's ancient history," she added, shaking her head.

Again, Hakeem detected sadness in her voice. He wanted to know more about her.

Suddenly, the voice of an elderly woman yelled from inside Anika's house.

"Anika!" the voice said.

"Uh oh, there goes my grandma again. She can't get down the stairs too well without me," Anika said, her face looking strained. "I love her, but sometimes, I just wanna run out that door and never come back."

Hakeem nodded, thinking about Savon and the summer ahead. "I know the feeling," he said.

"Anika!" the frail voice called again. "Where are you, girl?"

"One second, Grandma!" Anika yelled, heading toward the house and then turning back to Hakeem. "Well, I gotta go. Grandma needs me," she said quietly. "Besides, I'm sure we'll see each other again, you know, for my guitar lesson."

"Definitely," Hakeem replied, watching Anika disappear inside the blue house next door. As soon as she closed the door, Hakeem grabbed his notebook.

He glanced at the lines he had written for Darcy earlier in the evening. Then he turned to a new page and began writing.

This time, what he wrote was not just about Bluford or Darcy. It was also about Detroit and what had happened to him since he arrived.

But most of all, he noticed as he reread the pages later that night, it was about Anika, the first person to make him feel as if the move to Detroit might not be so bad.

Chapter 3

Hakeem woke up the next morning in a daze. For an instant, he thought he was home in his old bed and that the move to Detroit had been a bad dream. But then he noticed the unfamiliar posters and felt the uncomfortable bed-spring in his back and knew the move was all too real.

Reluctantly, Hakeem sat up and stretched. He heard the heavy, wet sound of snoring and glanced over at the bed across the room. Savon was asleep, buried under a layer of blankets. Only his foot was visible, poking out from beneath his blue sheet. Apparently, he had come in sometime after Hakeem had fallen asleep.

At least he's quiet for once, Hakeem

thought, enjoying the morning silence. A crumpled fifty-dollar bill lay on top of some papers on Savon's desk.

How did he get that? Hakeem wondered.

Savon grunted and turned over, violently pulling the sheet tight against his body. For an instant, he looked eerily like a corpse in a body bag. Hakeem shuddered at the image.

After showering and getting dressed, Hakeem headed downstairs. His father and Uncle James were sitting together at the dining room table. They were talking but stopped suddenly when they saw him. The look on Dad's face was grim.

"There's my man," Uncle James said, standing up and smiling broadly. "I was about to head up there and wake you, but your dad said you were tired from all that traveling."

"How you doin', Uncle James?" Hakeem said, hugging him. It had been years since he had seen his uncle. Uncle James was two years older than Dad, but he looked ten years younger. Seeing him was like looking at a snapshot of Dad taken before the chemotherapy— another reminder of the past Hakeem could not reclaim.

"I'm doin' all right," he said, grasping Hakeem for several long seconds. Hakeem felt like a child in his uncle's embrace. "I'm glad you got here safe and sound, and I like that you got up so early. Not everyone in this house is an early bird." Hakeem knew his uncle was referring to Savon, who was still sound asleep when Hakeem got out of the shower.

"Uncle James could use some help at the store, and I told him you were willing to lend a hand. He's about to head over there now, and I thought you might want to go with him," Dad said.

Hakeem knew he didn't have a choice. If his father were healthy, he'd help Uncle James without any hesitation. But with him still recovering, the job was Hakeem's.

"Hakeem, I can't do what I used to do, not now anyway. I'm expecting you to fill in for me, until I get better," he'd said. Since then, Hakeem had taken on many tasks around the house. He didn't mind helping, but the many jobs made him feel different from other people his age, kids who didn't have to save money for their parents, shop for groceries, take care of their sisters so Mom and Dad

could go to the hospital. Dad's request was the latest in a long list of jobs Hakeem got but never asked for.

"Sure, I'll help," Hakeem replied.

"That's my man," Uncle James answered, patting Hakeem on the shoulder.

Dad nodded, his tired eyes haunting Hakeem as he left the house with Uncle James.

The drive to the furniture store from Uncle James's house took only about ten minutes, most of which were spent waiting at traffic lights. The store, JR's Discount Furniture, sat in a strip mall bordered by Motown Liquors on one side and an Everything-for-$1 market on the other. The cracked asphalt parking lot was pocked with potholes and littered with broken glass.

As they neared the front door, Hakeem noticed that the entire storefront was hidden behind a thick metal screen.

"Me and Savon put this up about five years ago to protect the glass," Uncle James said, unlocking the screen and hoisting it over his head until it disappeared above him like a garage door. "It ain't easy doing business around here, but this is home, and I ain't going nowhere else," Uncle James added defiantly.

With the metal screen raised, Hakeem could see that the storefront was lined with thick glass panels facing the busy street. Each panel displayed giant letters that appeared to be hand-cut from neon pink paper. The sign nearest the door spelled out "Summer Sale! Sofas and Chairs 40% off." On the other side of the door, Hakeem noticed a smaller orange and black sign that read "Help Wanted."

Uncle James followed Hakeem's eyes. "It's hard to find decent help. I just fired a young man last week. He was unreliable, always callin' out sick," Uncle James explained as he unlocked the front door and stepped inside.

"Here it is, Hakeem. My home away from home," Uncle James said proudly, spreading his arm out as if the entire world were his. The store consisted of two main aisles that stretched back from the front door. On the right side were a few sofas and chairs; on the left, a series of kitchen and dining room sets. Right in the middle was a display set up to look like a real living room, complete with sofa, love seat, coffee table, and a large fake tree. Its leaves were coated with a layer of fuzzy gray dust.

Hakeem smiled, imagining his friend Tarah's reaction to the display. *"Now that is one sorry living room!"* she'd say. *"And who would want a giant dust tree in their house? You'd have to pay me to put that anywhere except the trash."*

"I started out in a tiny store a few blocks north of here," Uncle James said, interrupting Hakeem's thoughts. "I was just a few years older than you, working for an old guy who wanted to get out of the city. He sold his place to me. After working hard for a few years, I was able to move into this building where we got three times the space."

"Looks nice," Hakeem replied politely.

Outside, an ambulance raced past the store, its sirens fading in the distance. Uncle James looked up for a second but then continued.

"A lotta stores have closed or moved out over the past few years. Me, I'm stayin'. This neighborhood needs businesses. Kids need to see that there are ways of makin' a respectable living without gettin' involved in the garbage that

43

happens on these streets. Now if only I could get your thick-headed cousin to listen to me. All he wants to do is waste his time with his friends," Uncle James complained wearily, flipping on a light switch.

Hakeem didn't say a word. He wasn't sure how to respond. He had his own doubts about Savon, but he knew better than to share them with Uncle James. That would be asking for trouble.

"Listen, Hakeem," Uncle James said, pausing as if he were searching for something. "Your pops told me how you've had to be the man around the house since he got sick, so I am gonna talk to you man to man."

"Okay," Hakeem agreed, nervous about what his uncle had to say.

"Business's been a little slow this year, and I had to let people go. Now, I'm doing the work of three people," he explained. Hakeem could see that it was difficult for him to admit. "But I can handle that, especially with you around. Savon's the one I'm worried about."

"*Savon?*"

"I think he might be headed for trouble, and he don't listen to me or anybody anymore," Uncle James confessed. "I

44

was just hoping, now that you're here, you could keep an eye on him. Maybe talk some sense into him too."

"I can try, but—"

"And listen to me, Hakeem," Uncle James interrupted. "If you see anything that might be serious, you got to tell me, no matter what it is. I'm countin' on you."

Hakeem could not argue with his uncle's intense stare, but he wanted to. For months, he had struggled to help take care of his own family. Now, not only would he be doing that and helping his uncle; he was also to play big brother to Savon.

Savon hates me, Hakeem wanted to say, but Uncle James looked at him gravely, as if he were entrusting him with a great responsibility, something Hakeem could never question.

"Okay, Uncle James. I'll keep an eye on him," Hakeem agreed, though he felt as if he was being pulled into a trap he could never escape.

Nine hours later, Hakeem's mother arrived to take him home. Hakeem was grateful to see her. He didn't think he could stand another minute in the store.

In the morning, he had organized displays, packed up a chair, and helped unload two new sofas. In the afternoon, he had swept the aisles and scrubbed all the glass panels in the front of the store. It was as if Uncle James had saved work for months so he could make Hakeem do it.

"How was work today?" Mom asked as he collapsed into the passenger seat of Aunt Lorraine's beat-up Nissan.

"It was okay," he replied, releasing a deep sigh. His arms burned, his legs ached, and he felt as if he had run a marathon.

The drive back to the house took just a few minutes. As Hakeem wearily climbed the front steps, his mother put her hand on his shoulder. Her skin looked worn and thin in the late afternoon sun.

"You know, Hakeem, your dad and I are really sorry that we had to move you out here."

"I know, Mom."

"If there was any other way, we—"

"I know, I know," Hakeem insisted, unable to hide his frustration. He knew the trap he was in. He didn't need her to remind him again. "You told me a million times already. There's nothing you can do. And there's nothing I can do. I just gotta deal with things right now. Believe me, I understand."

"Understand what?" a voice cut in from inside the house. It was Dad, his forehead creased with concern. Hakeem's mother's hand dropped from his shoulder like a stone.

"Nothin', Pop," Hakeem said. For months, he had tried his best never to complain to his father. Dad had enough on his mind. "W-we were just talkin' about work stuff."

"Oh," his father replied. "Everything okay today?

"Yeah, Dad. Everything was fine."

"You sure, son?"

"I'm just tired, that's all. And hungry," he added, hoping to change the subject.

"Well, I think your aunt can take care of that," Dad said, stepping aside so Hakeem could get to the dining room.

Savon rushed out of the dining room just as Hakeem entered. The two nearly collided.

"Hey, cuz, you gonna take my seat at the dinner table too?" Savon mumbled so no one else could hear him. His eyes glared with fury.

"What?" Hakeem asked. He wasn't ready for his cousin, not now.

"Don't act surprised. You're already takin' everything else," he said with a scowl and then turned to his mother. "I'll be back later tonight, Mom. I gotta help Tariq with something," Savon said and then dashed out the door.

"Don't be back too late," Aunt Lorraine hollered, but Savon was already gone. "I swear that boy will give me an ulcer."

After dinner, Hakeem went upstairs, closed the door to the small bedroom, and collapsed on the bed. He wished he could go away, that no one would ask anything more of him. But then he heard a soft knock on the door.

"What?" he grumbled.

"What are you doing?" said a child's voice. It was his sister Charmaine.

"I'm minding my own business." It was what he usually said to his sisters when he didn't want to be bothered. But as soon as he said it, he felt guilty. He knew the adjustment to Detroit wasn't any easier on them. "Come on in."

Charmaine and Charlene opened the

door, walked in, and then sat on the bed next to him.

"How are you two doing today?" he asked.

"Fine," Charmaine said. She looked at her sister and giggled.

"What is it?" he asked, trying to be patient with them.

"We met this pretty girl next door, and she told us that you're supposed to teach her to play the guitar," Charlene said.

Hakeem smiled, remembering his talk with Anika. "Is that all she said?"

"She said you're cute, too," Charlene added and then started to laugh.

"Oh, no she didn't," Hakeem said.

"Yes she did," the girls replied together in between bouts of laughter.

"So what's so funny about that? That just means she's got good taste," Hakeem said, tickling them both. Their laughter cheered him up, reminding him briefly of home and a time when cancer was something he'd heard of on TV, not seen in his own house.

Moments later, Hakeem heard a voice downstairs and knew that Uncle James was home. "You did good work today, Hakeem," Uncle James yelled. "I hope you're getting your rest. We got a big shipment coming tomorrow, and I sure could use you."

Hakeem cringed at the idea of another grueling day at the store, but he knew Dad was listening to his every word.

"I'll be there," he said.

"Good. Don't stay up too late. You're gonna need your strength."

Without a word, the girls left the bedroom and closed the door.

Dreading the day to come, Hakeem changed out of his work clothes, stretched out on the bed, and fell into a deep dreamless sleep.

Chapter 4

"Let's go, Hakeem," Uncle James said, knocking on the bedroom door and jarring Hakeem from sleep. "We're going in early. The dollar store next door got robbed."

Hakeem opened his eyes, saw the clock, and groaned. It was 7:30, and every muscle in his lower back was sore from the previous day's work. *I wanna go home*, he thought.

Savon's mattress creaked, and he heard movement from the other side of the room. It was the second night in a row that Hakeem hadn't heard his cousin go to bed. Hakeem wondered how late Savon had been up. He was about to ask him when he noticed that Savon had grabbed a pillow and put it over his head.

Hakeem yawned, rubbed his eyes,

and headed to the shower.

A half hour later, Uncle James and Hakeem got to the store. A police car was pulling away when they arrived. An Asian man standing in front of the dollar store watched them closely as they approached.

"That's Mr. Sung," Uncle James said. "He owns the dollar store. He called me this morning about the robbery."

As soon as they got out of the car, Uncle James walked over to Mr. Sung, and the two began talking. Uncle James's face looked tense when he returned. "That's the third robbery around here in the past month," he said angrily. "I don't know what the cops are doing, but I got one of the only stores that ain't been robbed," Uncle James added. "I know we need it, but I can't afford no alarm system right now."

Hakeem and his uncle inspected the exterior of the store before going inside. Everything seemed undisturbed. Still Hakeem had an eerie feeling knowing that just hours earlier someone was creeping around in the dark. What if the person carried a gun?

Once the store opened, work was even worse than the day before. A new sign, painted on the glass by Uncle James, announced a "2-Day Sale" with "Huge Summer Discounts!" Hakeem was surprised to see that it attracted a steady stream of customers, which thrilled his uncle. But while Uncle James attended to customers, Hakeem mopped and scrubbed the rear of the store by himself. For hours, he worked on his knees, scraping the cement floor until it was bright and clean.

"The floor looks good, Hakeem," Uncle James said late in the day. "Last time it looked like that was when Savon cleaned it about six months ago. That was just before all this nonsense with his friends started. He ain't done much in here since. That boy don't know the meaning of work, not like you," he said.

Hakeem's jaws tightened at his uncle's words. Something about them made Hakeem feel dishonest.

"You and Savon get a chance to talk yet?"

"No, not yet. I been working whenever he's home," Hakeem replied, knowing that work wasn't the real reason the two weren't talking.

James nodded thoughtfully and said, "Why don't you take tomorrow morning off. Maybe you two can hang out or something."

"Are you sure?" Hakeem asked.

"Yeah, you earned it," Uncle James said, leaving to greet a customer.

Great, Hakeem thought, imagining a conversation with Savon. While time off sounded nice, a day with Savon seemed almost worse than a day of work.

"Your uncle is so pleased with your work," Aunt Lorraine gushed at dinner that night. "He said you learn fast and work hard."

"Thank you," Hakeem mumbled between bites of his cheeseburger.

"I see all the work at this store has increased your appetite," Mom said with a smile. "You keep working that hard, and you're gonna look like Savon."

Hakeem smiled uncomfortably and poured a glass of soda.

"Yeah, and hopefully *he'll* be a little more like Hakeem," Aunt Lorraine said. "I sure hope that boy gets his act together. He and James got into a big argument a few months back, and he's been walkin' around with a chip on his shoulder ever since. I know James is tough on him sometimes, maybe a little too tough.

But it's only cause he doesn't want Savon to get in trouble like so many of the kids around here. There ain't no use tellin' Savon that, though. He don't wanna listen to nobody."

"He's at that age," Mom spoke up. "This is when some of them start to rebel, except Hakeem. He's not that type," she said, smiling at him.

Hakeem wanted to get up and leave the table. He felt as if he were under a giant magnifying glass. Everyone talked about him as if they knew what he was thinking, yet no one had a clue.

Dad spoke up then, the lines in his forehead a bit deeper than usual. "It can't be easy on Savon havin' us here either, having to share his room and all. Maybe that has something to do with his behavior," he said.

"Henry, this started long before you arrived. He had been working at the store all the time, and then they had that argument, and something snapped. Now, it's like pullin' teeth to get him to help out. And with the friends he's got . . . I really worry."

"You ever try sittin' down and talkin' with him about it?" Dad asked.

"There's no talkin' to that boy right

now. He's hard-headed and so angry sometimes. I feel like I don't know my own son. Sometimes I feel like he's a stranger," Aunt Lorraine admitted, her voice trembling slightly.

Mom reached across the table to comfort her. "He's not a stranger," she said softly. "You just keep on loving him no matter how hard it gets at times. Keep loving him and he'll turn 'round."

"That's what I'm praying for," Aunt Lorraine replied. "I'm praying that he turns around before—"

Just then Savon opened the front door, carrying a plastic bag. Without a word, he quickly moved through the dining room and darted up the steps. Everyone watched him in icy silence.

Seconds later, the upstairs door closed with a muffled thud. The sound was followed quickly by the rhythmic bass of rap music thumping like a giant heartbeat in the ceiling overhead.

"You see what I mean?" Aunt Lorraine said.

Dad nodded thoughtfully.

Hakeem sighed and rubbed his temples, trying unsuccessfully to push away the headache that was beginning to creep into his skull.

After dinner, Hakeem reluctantly climbed the stairs to the bedroom. He had to get his guitar. Knowing Savon was in the room, he decided to be as quick as possible. Just rush in, get the guitar, and get out. There would be no words, no opportunity for confrontation. He'd save that for later, when he wasn't tired and his head didn't feel like someone was trying to hammer a rusty spike into his brain.

At the top of the steps, Hakeem paused outside the door and felt the heavy beat of the music. He rapped his knuckles against the wooden door, but the music continued. He knocked again, this time a bit louder. Still no response. Frustrated, he grabbed the doorknob and turned. It was locked.

"What's he doing?!" Hakeem growled under his breath.

Balling his hand into a fist, he pounded three times, making sure that the sound would be heard over the music. For an instant, Hakeem thought he heard shuffling inside. Then the music cut off.

"What?" Savon said from inside.

"It's me," Hakeem said. "I need to get something."

"I need some privacy right now," he said with an edge to his voice. "Why don't you go back downstairs, and talk about me some more. I'm leavin' soon, and you can go to bed then."

Hakeem seethed with anger. Staring at the closed door, he wanted to smash it into pieces and then pound Savon's face. He took a deep breath and struggled to regain his composure.

"Savon, I ain't playin' with you, man. Just give me my g-g-guitar. That's all I want."

For several long seconds, Hakeem stood in the hallway, unable to hear anything except the TV downstairs and the thud of his own heartbeat pounding in his temples. If he didn't get the guitar, there would be war.

Then the door opened.

Savon was wearing a Detroit Pistons jersey and had an expensive-looking silvery chain hanging from his neck. "Here you go, Cali. Go play another B-B-Beach Boys song," he mocked, holding out the guitar though the partially-opened door.

For an instant, Hakeem imagined himself smashing the instrument across Savon's face. He blinked back the image and grabbed the guitar.

Savon smirked, sucked his teeth, shut the door in Hakeem's face, and locked it. From the hallway, Hakeem heard him opening his closet door and moving things around. Then the music kicked on, and Hakeem was left standing in the hallway alone.

"You *better* close that door," Hakeem grumbled as he walked down the steps, his vision clouded by rage.

Outside on the back step, Hakeem let his frustration bleed through his fingers into the strings of his guitar. Slowly, the pain in his head eased, and his anger transformed into music, which dissipated into the evening air like steam.

The guitar allowed him to tell the truth his family didn't seem to understand, that he was scared for his father, that he missed his friends, that he wanted to go home, that he didn't know how to deal with Savon. Music and his journal were the only places he didn't have to be strong or silent.

When he finally stopped playing, the sky was dark, and cool damp air had replaced the heat of the day.

"I was wondering when you were going to take a break," said a familiar voice nearby.

Hakeem looked up to see Anika watching him from her yard.

"You come for another show?" he said with a smile.

"Actually, I was gonna ask you about that guitar lesson, but you looked so serious I decided to leave you alone."

"It's been a rough day," he admitted. "More like a rough week."

"I heard that," she replied sympathetically. "Seems like you and me are in the same mood."

Anika was silent for a second. Hakeem could see her bright eyes against the dark.

"Hey, you wanna go for a walk or something? I could go for a slice of pizza."

"That's the best thing I heard all day," he said, his mood lifting at her suggestion. "Show me the way."

Out on the street, Hakeem struggled not to stare at Anika. Her body was perfect. *A work of art wrapped in jeans and a black tank top,* Hakeem would write in his journal. Several times, he was nearly speechless as he looked at her smooth coffee skin, her full lips, her onyx eyes.

As they walked, the two of them

talked about their favorite music, TV shows, and movies. But when they sat down inside Metro Pizza, Anika's mood changed, and her eyes became more serious.

"So what do you think of Detroit?" she asked, raising a slice of pizza to her mouth.

Hakeem wiped a bit of melted cheese from his lip. "To be honest, I haven't even seen much if it. All the music and history here, and all I've seen is my uncle's store. This is the first time I been out without my uncle bossin' me around."

"You better get used to it if you're gonna keep working with Mr. Randall. That's just the way he is. Believe me, I know. Savon used to complain about it all the time. That store is your uncle's life," she replied.

Hakeem was bothered by the idea that Savon and Anika talked, but he kept his thoughts to himself.

"I'm starting to feel trapped there, and I've only worked a few days," he admitted. "I know I should be grateful and all. But it's hard, you know? And now there are these robberies," he said bitterly.

"*Robberies?*" Anika said, seeming surprised and interested at the same time.

"Yeah, the dollar store near my uncle's shop was robbed last night. He's so worried, he wants to have a security system put in. The police don't seem to have a clue who's doing it."

"Yeah, well, that doesn't surprise me. They're usually the last to know what's going on. There are so many thugs around here, they don't know where to look."

Hakeem looked at Anika as she spoke. There was a bitterness in her voice, but what also struck him was the word she used—*thugs*. It was the word he noticed on Savon's magazine earlier that day.

"Most of the boys I knew from school are in jail or they're on their way. Some of the girls ain't much better. They commit crimes to get money or respect. It's sad. I used to be into that, but no more. Now, I just wanna get outta here, you know."

Hakeem nodded. He knew what it was like to want to run away. He felt it too, now more than ever. "Where would you go? This is your home, right? And what about your grandma?"

"No, this is where my mom *left* me," Anika replied, an edge in her voice. "And soon, a social worker is gonna put my grandma in a nursing home. When that happens, all I'll have is my job at the laundromat, and that ain't enough for me. I got a cousin in California. That's where I'm headed."

Hakeem didn't know what to say. Anika had troubles far deeper than he realized. She wiped her eyes for an instant, as if dust had briefly irritated her. "You mean you're goin' to Cali'?" he said, doing his Savon impression.

She smiled. "I'm sorry to be dumping all my drama on you. You got your own troubles to deal with right now."

"It's okay, Anika," Hakeem replied, trying to think of something helpful to say. He had not expected their conversation to go this way. He stood close to her and put his hand on her back. "You ever think about college? That's my plan. I want to be a teacher."

"*College?*" Anika repeated. "With my grades, they'd laugh me right out the front door."

"Well, you seem pretty smart to me," he said.

"I got street smarts, Hakeem. That's not what they want in school."

"But—"

"Look, don't you start worrying about me. I know what I'm doing. I'm headin' to California. I just wish I got to know you sooner, Mr. Blues Man," she said with a smile. Her face seemed to recover its brightness, as if her words made her feel better. "Let's go home," she added, reaching down and grabbing his hand. He swallowed hard, trying to conceal his surprise.

"And just in case you were wonderin' about me and Savon," Anika spoke up, a glimmer in her eye. "We were together a while ago, but that's over."

"And what makes you think I was wondering about that?" Hakeem asked, pleased by what she said.

"Street smarts, remember?" Anika replied, pointing to her head as they walked out onto the street. She was somehow honest and secretive at the same time. He'd never met anyone like her. Yet as they crossed the street toward her house, she suddenly froze in her steps. "Oh no," she said, stepping away from him.

Hakeem looked up to see Savon

walking toward them. He was with two friends, and they were heading straight at them.

"Now I've seen everything," Savon said, shaking his head as if what he saw hurt and disgusted him. "I was hungry for some pizza, but now I feel sick to my stomach. Cuz, I gotta give you credit. You don't waste no time," he added.

"Savon, what's your problem?" Anika said. "You been buggin' for months now. I thought we were cool."

"We are cool. I ain't got no problems with you, girl. I'm just surprised my cousin's a player, that's all. What about Darcy, cuz?" Savon asked as he walked by. "I guess it ain't so hard to leave home after all."

Hakeem's blood boiled. How could Savon know of Darcy? He turned to Savon, but already his cousin was across the street, heading to Metro Pizza.

"Who you been talking to?" Hakeem asked, but Savon and his friends went inside with no reply.

"Just ignore him," Anika said. "He's just frontin' with you, that's all. I can tell."

"Seems more like he's trying to pick a fight with me."

"Him, no. He just acts that way so people leave him alone. When I first met him, he was heavy, and everyone teased him. Then he started liftin' and actin' hard so kids would respect him. It worked, I guess. But he ain't bad like the other kids around here. He just pretends to be."

"Well, if he's so good, why aren't you with him?"

"That's a long story for another time," she replied, looking away from him. Together, they walked several blocks toward the house in near silence.

At one point, Anika pointed out a small laundromat not far from Uncle James's house. "That's where I work," she said as they passed. "Come visit me there some time. It's so boring."

Hakeem fought to contain all the questions he had for her. And he still wondered how Savon knew about Darcy. There had to be some explanation. But what?

Finally, they stopped walking in front of Anika's house.

"So, it sounds like you got a girl back home," she said suddenly.

"A girl?"

"Yeah, you know, a *girlfriend*," she

said, locking her eyes on him.

Hakeem stammered, unsteady in her intense gaze. "The s-s-situation is real confusing."

"Is that the Darcy Savon was talkin' about?"

"Yeah, but we sort of broke up when I came here," he confessed, feeling a twinge of guilt as the words came out of his mouth.

"Do you miss her?"

Hakeem paused for a moment. Nervous energy trembled in his stomach. "Sometimes . . . but not right now," he admitted, feeling stupid for being so honest.

Anika smiled, bit her lip, and took a step back. "I'm lookin' forward to that guitar lesson."

"Me too," he replied, taking a deep breath.

"Goodnight, Hakeem," she said as she walked up the step to her front door, the words sounding to him like music.

"Goodnight," he replied, excitement and confusion waging a silent war deep in his chest.

Chapter 5

The minute he got inside, Hakeem headed upstairs. He wanted to see Anika again, yet he felt guilty, as if just thinking about her was somehow a betrayal of Darcy. He wondered if Darcy was dating someone else back home. The thought bothered him, but it did not push Anika from his mind. Her sad story echoed in his head like a catchy song.

But what bothered Hakeem most was Savon. How did he know about Darcy? Could he have talked to Mom and Dad? Probably not.

Then Hakeem noticed something unusual. His journal, which had been next to his bed, was missing. He glanced around the room and spotted it on top of a stack of entertainment magazines on Savon's desk. It was open and faced down, as if someone was reading it and had put it down to save the page.

Furious, Hakeem snatched the notebook from Savon's desk and glanced at the open page.

"*Dear Darcy, I'm scared about what's happening with my Dad . . .* ," he read. It was a note he had written to Darcy several weeks ago. The truth hit Hakeem like a punch in the stomach.

Savon had read his private writing!

"I can't believe he read my journal," Hakeem said out loud, kicking a new pair of Nikes Savon had left in the middle of the bedroom floor. "That's it, Savon," he growled. His cousin had gone too far this time. For an instant, something in Hakeem's mind snapped, and he saw the world in an angry red rage.

"That's it," he said again, opening Savon's closet. "Now let's see what *you're* hiding."

Hakeem leaned forward and scanned the piles of clothes, mysterious bags, and stacks of boxes in the closet. He grabbed a small shoebox from one of the piles.

Popping open the lid, he found a collection of old photographs. On top was a crumpled family picture of two young boys. Looking closely, Hakeem realized it was Savon and him. They were sitting on the front step together, each with his arms resting on the other's shoulder. But Savon had a hand behind Hakeem's head making a "V" with his thick fingers so that Hakeem appeared to have horns. Hakeem had never seen the picture. What struck him most about the photo was the smiles. Both he and Savon had wide, toothy grins. Hakeem couldn't remember feeling as happy as he looked in the picture.

"*What happened to us, Savon?*" he asked, feeling a wave of sadness for a time he could not reclaim. A time before cancer and moving. A time before he and his cousin learned to dislike each other. But the anger in his chest was stronger, and he put the pictures down and dug deeper.

In a second stack of photos, Hakeem found a wallet-sized picture of Anika. Its edges were worn and frayed. On the back, the words "From your fly girl" were written in rounded letters. Anika looked younger, and her hair was in braids. The shot might have been three or four years old, he guessed. Hakeem felt a wave of jealousy. He put the photos back and reached farther into the closet.

Along the back wall, Hakeem discovered an enormous stack of hip hop CD's. It was the biggest collection he had ever seen outside a music store. It had to cost hundreds of dollars, maybe more. *How could Savon afford so much music?* Hakeem wondered.

Just then, he heard footsteps from downstairs. It had to be Savon. Hakeem's hands began to sweat.

He quickly closed the box and put it back exactly as he'd found it. Then he quietly closed the closet door and crept back to his bed. The sound on the steps grew closer.

Hakeem grabbed his guitar and began playing it softly, pretending to concentrate.

There was a knock at the door. "Hakeem, are you awake?" came his mother's voice from the other side of the door. Hakeem shook his head and breathed a sigh of relief.

"Yeah, Mom. Come on in."

"Coop's on the phone," she said, opening the door.

"For real?" Hakeem replied, happily surprised. "Why's he callin' so late?"

"He forgot about the time difference.

It's only 8:30 in California. I told him you were in bed, but he said it was important."

Hakeem raced downstairs and picked up the phone in the kitchen.

"Coop!" he exclaimed.

"Wassup, yo?" Cooper began. "When your mom answered the phone, I was like 'What's he doin' in bed so early?' But I forgot about the time difference."

"Don't worry about it, Coop. I'm just glad to hear your voice, man. So what's goin' on? How are you and Tarah doin'?" Hakeem asked, eager to hear news from back home.

"We're fine. Tarah's on my back every day to take her here and there, just like she always was," Cooper said. "I been workin' real hard at the garage. Mr. Nye keeps promisin' me a raise, but I don't never see one. How's your pops?"

"I don't know, Coop," Hakeem confessed. "He still seems tired all the time. I get scared thinking about that next checkup. What if it comes back . . . you know?"

"You gotta keep the faith, bro. Your pop's a strong man. He'll be all right."

"I hope you're right," Hakeem replied. Cooper's words cut to the emotions

Hakeem hid from everyone else. For a minute, he struggled to tuck his feelings away where no one, not even Cooper, could see them. *Be strong*, he reminded himself.

"So what 'bout you? How's your summer goin'?" Cooper asked.

Hakeem leaned his back against the wall and looked to see if anyone was listening. Uncle James was asleep in his chair in front of the TV. Everyone else had gone to bed, except Savon, who hadn't come home yet.

"Busy, Coop. All I do is work. It's different around here too. The people, the neighborhood. It's only been a few days, I know, but man, I really miss home," Hakeem admitted.

"What about that cousin of yours?"

"Man, you don't even want to go there. The two of us don't mix, Coop. And I think he's headed for some serious trouble." As he spoke, Savon came in the front door. Hakeem turned around, lowered his voice, and spoke softly into the phone. "But I can't talk about that right now."

"You all right, bro?" Cooper asked.

"I'm fine," he said, glancing back to see Savon going upstairs. "So how's

73

Darcy? What's she up to?" There was a pause on Cooper's end.

"Coop? You there?"

"I have some bad news about Darcy," he answered somberly.

Hakeem felt a sinking feeling in his stomach. "What is it?"

"It's her grandma. She collapsed today, and now she's in the hospital. It doesn't look good. She's really weak."

Hakeem felt his entire body go numb. He knew how close Darcy had been to her grandmother. Normally, he would be there to comfort her, but now he was thousands of miles away. It was as if he was forced to watch an accident he could not prevent.

"Hak, you there?" Cooper asked.

"How's Darcy holding up?"

"She's with her family. Tarah and I are keeping an eye on her. She'll be okay."

"I wish I could be there for her right now."

"Bro, you got your hands full with your own problems right now," Cooper said. "Just take care of things, and I'll call you if anything changes. And remember what I said before you left. You got a place to stay here with me if you ever wanna come home. I mean it."

"Thanks, Coop," Hakeem said, wishing there was some way he could return home. "You're the best, man."

"Later, Hak."

Hakeem felt stunned when he hung up the phone. There were just too many things pulling him in too many directions. Inside he felt worn, as if his spirit had somehow been rubbed raw. Wearily, he climbed the steps to Savon's room, hoping his cousin was already asleep.

When he opened the bedroom door, Hakeem knew something was wrong.

Long eerie shadows stretched across the walls from floor to ceiling. They were cast by a dim lamp plugged in the far corner of the room. All the other lights in the room were out. Hakeem had never noticed the night-light, but even more unusual was the sound. The room was silent. Dead silent. The only noise Hakeem heard was the occasional whoosh of a passing car.

"Savon?" he whispered. There was no reply.

Hakeem turned on the light and scanned the room. The window at the foot of Savon's bed was wide open. A mound of pillows had been arranged and covered on the bed to look like someone was sleeping there. But with the light on, Hakeem could see through the disguise.

Savon was gone.

Hakeem examined the window. It faced the street, but it was directly over the roof of the house's front porch. The drop from the window to the porch was only a few feet. The porch roof connected to a black iron railing that could easily be climbed. Savon must have climbed out the window. Looking down at the street, Hakeem was sure it wasn't the first time Savon had used the window to get out of the house. That explained how during the past few nights he never heard his cousin climb the noisy stairs to bed.

But where did Savon go, and what was he doing out this late? Hakeem wondered.

Whatever it was, Hakeem concluded, it wasn't good. He considered waking Uncle James and telling him immediately. But he knew it would create a huge scene. Everyone would wake up, including his parents. Perhaps someone would even call the police. Hakeem didn't feel that all that was necessary, especially since he suspected it was not the first time Savon had crept out in the dark. He decided to wait. If Savon wasn't back by morning, he'd tell everyone.

Drained by the day's events, Hakeem changed for bed and stretched out on his lumpy mattress. The minute his head hit the pillow, he fell into a fitful sleep. At one point, he dreamt he was playing his guitar for Anika on the back porch. But in the dream, Darcy was watching them from a distance and crying, a sound that was louder than the guitar music. The dream startled him enough that he woke up and glanced at the clock. It was 3:07 a.m. The room was still quiet, but then Hakeem heard something.

First there was a dull thud, then a slight metallic rattle followed by the sound of something scampering. Hakeem looked at the window and watched Savon's face appear in the glow of the dim night-light. He wore a black do-rag around his head as he climbed like a thief through the window. Immediately he unplugged the night-light. Hakeem couldn't believe his eyes.

In the dim shadows of the darkened room, Savon quietly put something in his desk drawer and changed his clothes. Within minutes, he was in bed. Hakeem listened as his cousin's breathing grew steadily deeper and turned into a gentle snore.

Annoyed and exhausted, Hakeem rolled over and faced the wall. He tried to imagine what Savon was doing and what he would say to Uncle James in the morning.

Could it be that Savon was seeing a girl somewhere? Probably not. There'd be no reason to be so secretive about that. And what about the CDs, new shoes, and unexplained money? They had to be connected.

Suddenly, something clicked in Hakeem's mind.

The robberies.

Maybe Savon had something to do with all the stores that had been robbed in the area. The idea made complete sense. Savon was out the night the dollar store was robbed. Savon's involvement would also explain why Uncle James's store was spared. No wonder he had the dark clothes, the mysterious schedule, the money, and the jewelry.

Savon was a thief.

The shock of the idea hit Hakeem in

waves, fighting for a while the sleep that tugged irresistibly at his eyelids.

At 9:00, Hakeem awoke dreading the day ahead of him. He was tired. It was as if he hadn't slept at all. He could not imagine what he would say to Uncle James today. To Savon.

In the daylight, the events of the previous night seemed cloudy and dreamlike. Maybe he had dreamed that Savon was sneaking around in the dark or that Darcy's grandmother was sick. But he knew he was fooling himself. He had learned when Dad fell ill that good things in life usually turned out to be fake, like Santa Claus. But unpleasant things, like cancer, were almost always too real.

At least I don't have to work, Hakeem thought. It was the morning Uncle James had given him off so he could talk to Savon. That idea seemed like a joke now. If what he saw last night was true, Hakeem knew he should talk to Uncle James, not Savon. Still, what if what he had seen was somehow innocent? There was no way to know for sure unless he had proof.

As Hakeem debated what to do,

Savon snorted, rubbed his face, and got up. Without a word, he yawned and headed to the bathroom.

Alone in the room, Hakeem glanced at Savon's desk. The night before, he remembered his cousin had put something in the top drawer before he went to sleep. Eyeing the desk, he wondered what it was.

Hakeem listened. He could hear water running in the bathroom. Savon was probably brushing his teeth. That meant he still had a few minutes before he returned.

Jumping out of bed, Hakeem rushed to the desk and opened the top drawer. It was filled with CD's, a few silver chains, an old watch, some pens, and several notebooks. Running his hands into the back of the drawer, he felt a curious bundle of papers wrapped in rubber bands. He grabbed the bundle and looked. It was a folded wad of cash an inch thick.

Hakeem's eyes widened in surprise. Savon *was* the robber.

Through the walls, he heard the abrupt clunk of the pipes, signaling that the water had been turned off. Savon would be back in seconds. He shoved the money back and closed the drawer. He had to face Savon. Now.

Hakeem heard footsteps coming up the hall. He took a deep breath and braced himself.

"Savon, we need to talk," he said as soon as his cousin entered.

"Huh?"

"I saw you come in the window last night," Hakeem said,

"Man, get outta my face," Savon said, rolling his eyes. "You trippin'."

"I know what you are up to—"

"You don't know jack about me!" Savon roared, the veins in his neck bulging.

"I saw you put the money in your desk. I know—"

"*What* do you know?" Savon challenged, stepping closer to Hakeem.

"I know enough to see that you are headed for trouble."

"*Why*? 'Cause I don't come home early? 'Cause I won't spend another summer working at the store with my Dad? Or is it 'cause I ain't Mr. Perfect like you, *cuz*?" Savon stretched the last word out as if it was a curse.

"Savon, I'm tryin' to help you, man."

"I don't need your help! You think

you're better than me. That's what this is all about," he hissed. "You can take your help and your guitar back to California for all I care."

Savon's words hit Hakeem like a slap in the face. He'd done nothing wrong. He was trying to help, and yet *he* was being treated like the bad guy.

"Man, you are the biggest punk I know, Savon," Hakeem said, unable to restrain his own anger any longer.

"What'd you say?"

"You think I like sharing this room with you? You think I wanted to leave my friends to be here? You think I like that my dad's sick, and we lost our house?" Hakeem fumed, his hands shaking, the frustration of the past weeks spilling out like venom. "No, Savon, you didn't think of any of that, 'cause all you can think about is *you.*"

"Boy, you better *shut* your mouth!" Savon exclaimed, moving his face inches from Hakeem's.

"Oh, so now you're gonna threaten me, right?" Hakeem challenged, his frustration at the past month's events fueling his anger. "You haven't done nothing except dis me since I got here. Go ahead, hit me," he goaded, shoving

Savon back away from his face.

"That's it!" Savon barked, charging Hakeem like an enraged lion.

Chapter 6

Savon slammed his shoulder into Hakeem's chest, sending him crashing against the far wall of the bedroom.

The impact ignited the flame of Hakeem's rage into an all-out firestorm. Balling his hands into fists, he punched Savon, once in the stomach and once just above the eye, the blows fueled by anger at his cousin and at the events of the past year. Both times, his knuckles struck with a solid wet thud.

But Savon was fast. He responded with an arching punch that landed like a brick against Hakeem's cheek. The impact made Hakeem's ears ring and his legs buckle.

And Savon kept coming.

Surging forward like a linebacker, he tackled Hakeem, dragging him to the ground with enormous force.

In blind fury, Hakeem slammed his elbows and fists into Savon, trying unsuccessfully to free himself from his cousin's grasp.

"What's going on in there?!" Uncle James's voice thundered.

Hakeem and Savon froze as the bedroom door opened.

"Nothin', pop," Savon said, instantly letting go of Hakeem. "We just messin' around."

"Don't you lie to me, boy. I've about had it with you," Uncle James bellowed, barging into the bedroom. Hakeem's father was right behind him. "Y'all are cousins. Y'all are family. Blood is thicker than anything else. And family shouldn't be fightin' like that. Now Hakeem, go downstairs."

Hakeem's face burned with shame, and his cheek began to throb.

"But Uncle James, I started it."

"Don't try to cover for him, Hakeem. I know what's goin' on around here."

"But Uncle James—

"But *nothin'*. Just do as your uncle says," Dad ordered. Hakeem hurried out of the room as Uncle James approached Savon.

"Boy, I am embarrassed to call you my son right now. You don't do nothin' around here but disappoint me," Uncle James roared. "You got anything to say for yourself?"

"We was just playin' around, that's all," Savon replied. "Things got outta hand."

Uncle James slammed the bedroom door closed, but Hakeem could hear his uncle's raised voice in the hallway.

"I could deal with you ignorin' me, leavin' the store, and wastin' your summer with your friends, but I'm not about to let you turn this house upside down," he hollered. "There's gonna be some changes around here starting right now."

"Let's go," Dad said, leading Hakeem downstairs.

Uncle James' voice boomed through the walls. Hakeem felt a stab of guilt as he slumped in a chair at the dining room table. Not only had he failed to do what his uncle had asked; he had started a fight with his cousin. What bothered Hakeem more was that Savon didn't even try to blame him. Instead, he denied what happened.

Embarrassed to call you my son. The

words echoed in Hakeem's mind. They were like weapons, more harmful than fists.

The yelling upstairs continued like a storm overhead. Dad took a deep breath, crossed his arms and leaned against the wall of the dining room. At one point, Hakeem heard a thud from upstairs, followed by an even angrier outburst.

Hakeem lowered his head, wishing he could block the sound from his ears. He could feel his father's eyes boring into him.

"Dad, I'm sorry," he said, seeing the strain in his father's weathered face. "I just lost it."

His father sighed and shook his head, pausing as if speaking was a great effort. "All of us been through too much these days. I see you walking around like you got the weight of the world on your shoulders. I know you're angry at what's happened. I am too," he admitted, sniffling slightly. "But if I learned anything since I got sick, it's that life is too short for fightin', Hakeem. The world is already full of enough bad things. We don't need to waste our time making it worse, especially not with the people in our family."

Hakeem's face burned with shame. "I know, Dad. I'm sorry," he muttered.

"Now listen to me. Tomorrow is my checkup. Doctor's gonna test me to see if the cancer is still in remission. No matter what happens, your mother and I need you to be strong right now. So I am only going to ask you this once. Can you and Savon settle this yourselves?" Dad asked, his face firm and serious, his eyes unblinking.

Hakeem's mind snagged on his father's words. *Be strong.* The advice pained his ears. Inside he didn't feel like he had any strength left, not for Detroit or Savon or anything. *I'm tired, Dad,* he wanted to say. But how could he?

And what about Savon?

Hakeem had no idea what to do with him. For some reason, Savon refused to even blame him for starting the fight. Probably because he was protecting himself, Hakeem guessed. By taking the blame for the fight, Savon never gave Hakeem the chance to reveal the hidden money. But what if Savon refused to point a finger at Hakeem for another reason?

And what about the money? It probably came from robbing stores, Hakeem thought, but he wasn't absolutely sure. Savon's words were rude, but there was something else to them. Something sad. Listening to Uncle James yelling in the distance, Hakeem could not bring himself to tell Dad or anyone else what he knew. Not yet. Not if it involved Savon getting in more trouble for something he didn't do. One way or another, Hakeem had to find out how Savon had gotten so much cash. And if it turned out that Savon was the thief, he would tell everyone then. Not a moment before.

"Yeah, Dad," he replied finally, trying unsuccessfully to meet his father's gaze. "It's like Savon said. Just a misunderstanding. No big deal."

"You sure?" Dad asked, moving closer.

The back of Hakeem's neck began to sweat. His heart pounded like a piston.

"Yeah, I'm s-s-sure," Hakeem said, trying his best to avoid his father's tired stare.

Hakeem left the house an hour early. He could not look at his father, knowing the lie he had told. And he could not stand to be around Savon, who sulked in his room long after Uncle James left.

While Hakeem got dressed, Savon

refused to acknowledge him. Instead he sat on his bed almost zombie-like, his body completely motionless. Hakeem tried twice to talk to him, but Savon put a Walkman on and turned it up so loud that Hakeem could hear it in the hallway.

Hakeem headed straight to the laundromat Anika had pointed out the night before. She was the one person he could talk to. Glancing in the glass window, he spotted Anika inside talking to a tall wiry young man with a sharp, angular face. Hakeem had seen the face before, the day his family arrived at Uncle James's house. It had made him uneasy.

Inside the laundromat, a row of pale yellow washing machines thumped and shook loudly. A number of people sat in plastic chairs opposite the machines. A few were reading magazines. One was sleeping. Anika was in the back involved in an intense conversation with the stranger. Hakeem walked back to meet her.

"I told you. I can't do this anymore, Rasul," Anika said to the man. "I don't want any part of it."

"Girl, why you trippin'? This ain't nothin' new."

"I'm out, Rasul," Anika said, moving

her hands as if she was pushing something away. "You hear me? *Out.*"

"Hi, Anika," Hakeem cut in, sensing she was in trouble.

"Hakeem!" she exclaimed, surprise on her face.

"Who's this?" Rasul asked, staring Hakeem up and down.

"Rasul, this is . . . my cousin, Hakeem," Anika answered before Hakeem could speak. "He's visiting for a couple days."

Rasul's eyes narrowed slightly, but then he stepped back. "Anika, I'll catch up with you later," he said, turning and walking away.

Hakeem watched as he quickly left the laundromat.

"What's all that about?" Hakeem asked.

"It's a long story, Hakeem. Rasul's my ex-boyfriend, and he's still trying to get back together with me," she said quickly, her eyes darting rapidly as she spoke. "I hope you don't mind me calling you my cousin. It just made things easier. When Rasul gets jealous, he can get ugly," she added.

Hakeem studied her face. He didn't know whether to believe her. She looked nervous and uncomfortable. And he didn't like the way Rasul eyed him just before he left. "You all right?"

"I'm fine," she said. "He just gets on my nerves sometimes. Anyway, what are you doin' here? I thought you'd be at your uncle's store."

"I'm on my way there now. I just thought I'd stop by and see if you were here."

"What happened to your face?" she said, pointing to where Savon had punched him.

"Me and Savon got into a fight," he admitted.

"Oh my God! I can't believe he hit you," she said, running her hand near the welt on his face. "I know that boy has a big mouth, but he don't go around hurtin' people. At least he didn't used to."

"He didn't this time either. I pushed him first," Hakeem admitted. "I feel bad now 'cause Uncle James was really rough on Savon."

"You try to talk to Savon about it?"

"I did, but he wouldn't let me. I shouldn't have shoved him, Anika, but he got me so mad that I lost it," Hakeem grumbled, angry at himself.

"Believe me, I know about that. Back

in the day, Savon was always on my case, tryin' to tell me who I shouldn't be friends with and which places I shouldn't go. He was bossin' me just like his father bossed him. Finally we broke up 'cause all we did was fight all the time," Anika explained.

Hakeem felt his eyes twitch. He didn't like to hear about Anika and Savon, though he was curious. Even if it was old news, it still bothered him, adding jealousy to the sour mix of emotions he had for his cousin. Through the corner of his eye, Hakeem noticed the time on a dusty wall clock. "I gotta go."

"I'm glad you came to visit me," Anika replied, her eyes pulling him out of his thoughts. "Maybe we can see each other later. That is, if you're not too busy."

Hakeem could not help but smile. "I'll see if I can fit you in my schedule," he teased.

"Call me," she said, grabbing his hand and writing on it. "Here's my number."

"Girl, you're crazy," he said looking at the ink on his palm.

"Call me later," she said with a wave and a smile.

At 4:00, Hakeem leaned against a dumpster in the back of the furniture store. He had just loaded a sofa onto a truck, and he was taking a break.

He and Uncle James had barely spoken all day. Once Hakeem had tried to apologize for what happened, but Uncle James had cut him off before he could really say anything.

"No, Hakeem, I'm the one who is sorry. I asked you to keep an eye on him, and I shouldn't have done that. You were just trying to do what I told you. You got nothin' to apologize for," he had said.

"But I pushed him first."

"Hakeem, you don't have to stick up for him. I know what happened."

"I'm not, Uncle James."

"Hakeem, it's done. Savon isn't going to hit you again, not while he's livin' under my roof. And he ain't gonna leave the house for a week either. The time inside will do him good. He's got a lot of thinkin' to do," Uncle James insisted. "Maybe then, he'll get his butt back in the store where he belongs."

Hakeem wanted to protest, but he could see Uncle James had made up his mind. And when several customers walked in, Uncle James left him without another word. Business, it seemed, always came first. Frustrated, Hakeem busied himself in the back of the store and stayed out of Uncle James's way.

Still, he had a queasy feeling about Uncle James's decision. It meant Savon would be in the house all the time. And he was almost certain to be even angrier than before.

And what about Savon sneaking out the window each night? Uncle James knew nothing about that. Hakeem was sure Savon would do it again. Especially tomorrow, Friday night, the time Savon and his friends had made plans. The same day Dad was going to the doctor.

Hakeem shuddered with a growing sense of dread, a feeling that increased as the day wore on.

"Look at your face," Mom exclaimed when she picked up Hakeem at work. She, Aunt Lorraine, and his sisters had not been home when the fight broke out. They had left early for a full day of sightseeing in the city. "What did he do to you?"

"Nothin', Mom. I'm fine," he replied, feeling his swollen cheek. "We just had an argument, that's all."

"Well your father told me that, but he didn't say nothin' about your face."

"Just don't say anything to Savon, okay? That will only make things worse," he said, leaning back in the seat and trying to hide the bruised part of his face.

"That cousin of yours doesn't give me a good feeling at all," Mom said, driving the car out of the parking lot. They passed two young men walking by the small shopping plaza. One of the guys was Anika's friend Rasul. He pointed toward the dollar store as he walked.

"Well, he won't be going anywhere for a week at least," Hakeem said. "Uncle James grounded him."

His mother nodded and then turned to him. "You two gonna be okay in that room by yourselves?"

"Yeah, we'll be fine," he lied, telling her what he thought she wanted to hear.

"Say your prayers for your dad tomorrow. I'm worried about what the doctors might find," his mother admitted.

"I will, Mom," he said, avoiding her eyes again, fear lurking in his own heart.

As they parked in front of the house, Hakeem's pulse quickened. He wished he could avoid Savon, but he knew there was no way. He had to try to make peace with him.

On the front porch, Hakeem heard the sounds of his sisters' laughter followed by the sound of Savon's voice coming from inside the house.

"I told you you were rugrats. Two little rugrats from California," Savon said amidst the girls' giggling.

Hakeem opened the front door to see Savon sitting on the couch tickling Charmaine and Charlene, who rolled gleefully on the floor to escape him. All three of them stopped as soon as Hakeem entered.

"What happened to your face?" Charmaine asked.

"You got a big bruise right there," Charlene added, pointing to it.

Savon stood up suddenly, and headed up the stairs.

Hakeem cringed, looking for a way to escape their questions.

"Would you mind your own business and leave your brother alone," Mom jumped in. "He bumped his face at work today."

The girls seemed satisfied with their mother's explanation, though they stared at his bruise as if their eyes were glued to it somehow. Without waiting for more questions, Hakeem followed his cousin up the stairs.

Savon was sitting at his desk, writing something in a notebook, when Hakeem entered.

"I'm sorry for pushing you," Hakeem said, the words rushing awkwardly out of him. "And I'm sorry your dad punished you. He wouldn't listen to me when I tried to tell him what happened."

"Man, I don't need your apology," Savon said, his voice heavy with resentment. "You can take that someplace else, 'cause I ain't havin' it."

Hakeem closed the door. "Look, Savon, I don't know what you're into—"

"That's right! You don't," Savon barked. "So just stay outta my business."

"Savon, your dad's the one who told me to keep an eye on you," he cut back, trying to explain himself. "I didn't tell him, but I know you're planning to sneak out tomorrow night."

"Man, I don't care what my dad said. You ain't my babysitter!" Savon countered, his face an expression of outrage. "This is *my* house, *my* room. You already got my parents treating you like the son they wished they had. And now you gonna try to control *my* life too?" Savon's voice wavered slightly. "Yeah, I got plans on Friday, and I'm gonna keep 'em. I got to! Not you, not Dad, not anyone is gonna stop me. Just keep your mouth shut and stay outta my face!"

Savon turned on his stereo and cranked up the volume.

Hakeem was speechless.

Chapter 7

At dinner, the table was uncomfortably quiet. The metal clink of silverware was the only real sound during the meal.

Hakeem could see the worry in his parents' faces as they ate. He knew they were thinking about tomorrow. He was too.

Next to them, Savon ate as if the pork chop on his plate was an enemy, stabbing his fork into it in tense silence. Even Charlene and Charmaine were subdued, eyeing everyone nervously as if they sensed that talking was bad.

Hakeem considered alerting the family to Savon's plan, but he couldn't bring himself to do it. The idea of another clash with Savon made his head ache with stress. He could not imagine how the two would survive another day, let alone the whole summer or longer. But all that wouldn't matter if Dad's check-up turned out to be bad. Then his whole world would melt away.

Be strong, he told himself, the words seeming hollow and unhelpful. He wished he could see his friends.

When Uncle James came home complaining about kids in the neighborhood, Hakeem excused himself from the table. He had to get out. There was only one person he could go to.

Hakeem grabbed a phone and dialed the faded number on his palm. The phone rang several times before it was answered.

"Hello," Anika said sternly, as if the word itself annoyed her.

"Anika?" Hakeem said. "It's me, Hakeem."

There was a brief pause.

"Oh, Hakeem! I'm sorry. I thought you were someone else," she said. Hakeem could hear her repositioning the phone. "What's up? You sound bad."

"Rough day. I was hopin' we might do that guitar lesson tonight." Hakeem said, praying she would agree. Anything to get out of the house.

Again, Anika was quiet for several seconds. He wondered who she expected. Rasul, he guessed.

"I can't go anywhere now. I'm here with my Grandma," she said. There was another pause. "But if you want, you can come over."

Hakeem sighed in relief. "I'll be right there," he said.

Racing back upstairs, he grabbed his guitar and notebook, afraid to leave it with Savon again, and headed out. Seconds later, he walked up the concrete steps to Anika's porch and knocked on the door. Then he heard the click and snap of the door being unlocked.

"Hi, Hakeem," Anika said as the door opened. She eyed the street cautiously as she greeted him. "Come in. My grandma's upstairs sleeping, but it's okay. She can't hear us, not without her hearing aid." Anika's voice trailed off as she spoke.

Hakeem stepped into the front room of the house. It was the same shape and size as his aunt and uncle's living room, though it seemed much older. The air felt slightly musty, and the furniture was worn and faded. A collection of family pictures lined the wall, but most were yellowed with time. One was a black and white photo of a man in a military uniform standing proudly in front of the American flag.

Near the front door was one picture that looked more recent then the others. It depicted a round-faced woman who appeared to be in her thirties standing with her arms out. Behind her was the glistening ocean. She had a friendly smile.

"That's my cousin in California, the one who's waitin' for me," Anika said, locking the front door. "That beach is not far from her house," she added, gazing at the picture as if it were some perfect place. A promised land.

Hakeem thought the beach in the picture resembled one he and Darcy used to visit before the world turned upside down. Before the cancer. "Reminds me of home," he said, old memories flickering and fading in his mind.

Anika studied him closely, her almond eyes dark and mysterious. Looking at them, Hakeem could almost forget the last two weeks.

"Come with me," she said. "Come with me to California. You know you wanna go back home."

"Girl, are you serious?"

"I gotta get outta here, Hakeem," she confessed. "There's just too much drama here for me right now."

Hakeem nodded at her words. He could see she meant what she said, and he understood. He felt exactly the same way since he left home. "Is it Rasul?" he asked bluntly, unable to hide his curiosity. "I saw him tonight near my uncle's store."

Anika lowered her head and rolled her eyes, confirming his suspicion. "You don't even want to go there," she said. "Put it this way. The only thing I like around here these days is that guitar of yours."

"And not me?" he teased. Anika laughed slightly, her smile attracting him like a magnet. The time with her was like an oasis from his family.

"Maybe just a little," she said, running her fingers through her hair. "So when are you gonna teach me how to play?

"Are you sure you're ready? I require my students to be dedicated," he said, pretending to be serious.

She rolled her eyes and gave him a mock scowl.

"Okay. Sit down," he instructed.

Anika sat on the edge of the faded couch, and Hakeem sat beside her, his leg against hers. Putting his notebook down, he took the guitar and placed it gently on her lap so that it rested on her thigh. He suddenly got nervous. He had never been this close to any girl except Darcy.

"Now I'm gonna position your hands," he explained, trying to stay calm. Carefully, he reached around her back and took her left hand. His fingers trembled slightly. Her skin was soft and warm, and she watched him curiously as he placed the neck of the guitar against her palm. Then, with his heart racing, he took her other hand and placed it on the face of the guitar in front of her stomach.

Sitting so close to Anika, he could smell her hair and feel her breathing. He wanted to kiss her, but he wasn't sure how she'd respond.

"To play, you have to hold these fingers down," he said, slowly pressing her fingers against the guitar's neck. "And you play the strings like this." He dragged her hand across the strings, and the guitar sang a jumbled chord.

Anika laughed at the sound and

leaned back into him. Hakeem's heart skipped with excitement, and he laughed with her. Then, as he began to instruct her in a real note, he felt her breath against his neck and realized she was looking at him, not the guitar. Turning toward her, he felt her lips meet his for an instant.

"Now you have to teach me a song," she said, turning her attention back to the guitar.

Gradually, he taught her to play a blues chord and then another. After an hour, she could slowly alternate among three simple sound combinations. She seemed thrilled.

"See that? You're a natural," Hakeem said as she showed off what she learned.

Being with her was better than music, lifting him from his worries and distracting him from the day's pain and frustration. But as the evening wore on, his thoughts returned to the present. He dreaded what tomorrow would bring and the thought of spending the summer in Uncle James's house. Anika seemed to sense his thoughts.

"You never answered me before," she said, putting the guitar down. "About California."

"Are you sure you have to leave?"

"Yeah, I am. When the state puts my grandma in a nursing home, they're gonna put me in a foster home for six months, 'til I turn eighteen. I just can't do that," she said sadly. "Just come with me! The two of us could disappear. I got money for your bus ticket," she said, her eyes hopeful and sincere.

For an instant, with her next to him, the idea seemed perfect. But when he thought of his family, he knew he could not abandon them. And then there was school, something Anika seemed to have given up on. Her idea sounded nice, but it was a dream, an escape maybe, but not for him. "I can't leave my family, Anika. Not like that, especially not now. Are you sure there's no one here for you? Not even a friend?"

"*No*," she said firmly, twisting away from him and getting up. "They're the ones I'm trying to get away from." The thud of a car door outside suddenly startled her. She peered out a window and then turned to him. "It's getting late. You should probably go home before *your* family starts to worry." The storminess he had seen in her eyes returned.

Hakeem stood up, surprised by the sudden change in her mood.

"I'm sorry, Anika," he said at the door.

"It's okay," she said. "Don't worry about it."

"I'll call you tomorrow," he said.

"Okay," she said blankly. "Goodbye." She locked the door behind him.

It was 10:30 when Hakeem stepped back in his uncle's house. He knew his sisters and mother would be in bed, but he was surprised to see Uncle James and Dad talking when he entered. They stopped talking and stared at him when he closed the door. Dad's jaws were tight. Hakeem knew they had been having a serious talk.

"So," Uncle James said unnaturally, raising his eyebrows and forcing a smile. "How is Anika this evening?"

"She's fine," Hakeem replied, suddenly feeling as if he was under a spotlight.

"That's one pretty girl, Hakeem, but she's trouble. Her grandmother's been trying to control her for years, but she runs in a bad crowd, that one. She got busted shoplifting a few times, even

when Savon was datin' her. He tried to help her, but she even drove *him* crazy. Calling all the time. Always needin' something. But that was a few years ago. Hopefully she grew outta that, but I wouldn't know 'cause she doesn't talk to us much anymore," Uncle James said.

Hakeem squirmed inside. It felt strange to hear Uncle James talk about Anika, especially considering how little he knew his own son.

"She seems fine to me," he said, feeling the need to defend her. "She wanted a guitar lesson, so I taught her how to play a few chords."

"Umm hmm," Uncle James raised his eyebrows, nodded, and looked at Hakeem with a devilish grin.

"Leave him alone, James," Dad said. "Your uncle's just playin' with you. I'm glad you found someone here, you know, now that you can't see Darcy."

Hakeem took a deep breath but said nothing. Even though his father meant well, the comment stung. Dad's words made Darcy seem like an old light bulb, something he could just toss away and replace. The truth was that he had broken up with Darcy because he had to move away. Their relationship was

another victim of Dad's cancer, something else Hakeem knew he could never mention or complain about even though it ached like an old wound.

"Thanks, Dad," he said finally, trying to hide his sarcasm. "Savon upstairs?" Hakeem knew Savon would be there, but he wanted to change the subject.

"Yeah, he said he wanted to go to bed early."

"You all right, son?" Dad asked as Hakeem reached the steps.

"Yeah, I'm just tired," he replied going up the stairs, hoping Savon was already asleep.

Tired of all of you.

Hakeem's jaw dropped as soon as he entered the bedroom. The room was dark, the window was open, and the pillows had been arranged again to look like a sleeping person. But Savon was gone.

Hakeem cursed under his breath. He had expected Savon to sneak out again, but not on the very first night of his punishment.

Turning on the light, he put his guitar down and walked over to his bed. A sheet of notebook paper was on

his pillow. It contained one sentence of handwritten text.

DON'T SAY A WORD.

Hakeem crumbled the paper and threw it at Savon's desk. He hated being forced to lie to the family, but he didn't feel right telling them the truth. Something about Savon's words haunted him. They were just too desperate.

"You already got my parents treating you like the son they wished they had. And now you gonna try to control my life too . . . I got plans on Friday, and I'm gonna keep 'em. I got to!"

He couldn't tell them until he was sure of exactly what Savon was into. And, no matter what happened, he would find out tomorrow night.

After washing his face and brushing his teeth, Hakeem closed the bedroom door and turned off the light. On his way to bed, he glanced out of Savon's window.

"Tomorrow this ends, Savon," he said, scanning the street. There was no sign of Savon. But next door, a large gray sedan pulled away. It had been parked in front of Anika's house.

Hakeem thought he saw someone in the backseat, but in glare of the streetlights, he couldn't tell. The sedan turned at the corner of the street and disappeared. As the hum of its engine faded, the block grew still and quiet.

Hakeem stretched out uneasily on his mattress and said a prayer, his mind restless long into the night.

Chapter 8

Hakeem woke up the next morning to a dreary sky. The room was cool, and the sunlight that usually spilled through Savon's window was replaced by a dull gray glow.

Savon, Hakeem noticed as he glanced at the breathing mound of blankets, didn't seem to mind. He slept soundly, as if the events of the previous day had never happened. A new pair of shoes, thick black boots, were on the floor next to the bed. A stack of brand new CD's was on his desk. It seemed Savon was always buying something.

But with whose money? Hakeem thought bitterly.

Downstairs, Hakeem poured a bowl of cereal and tried to hide his worries.

"You and Savon getting along any

better?" Dad asked, sitting next to him. "Any problems last night?"

"We're cool," Hakeem replied, between spoonfuls of his cereal. The lie was automatic, but for now he didn't care. Until he found out what the doctor said, Hakeem felt like his life was stuck on hold somehow. It was as if an invisible bomb, cancer, was falling and everyone was waiting to see where it landed. Until he was sure, Hakeem would lie about Savon, his feelings about the move, his sadness about his friends. Anything to keep the peace.

Besides, he could see that his father was completely distracted. Sitting across the table, he stared blankly at his plate, his eyes focused on something no one else could see.

Upstairs, Hakeem hurried to get dressed as Savon slowly woke up.

"So, you seein' Anika?" he mumbled sleepily, his head partially hidden by his pillow. "How is she?"

"What do you care?" Hakeem challenged, feeling a ripple of jealousy for Savon and the past he had with Anika.

"You just better watch yourself, cuz," Savon said with a yawn. "That girl's bad news. She runs in the wrong crowd. She steals stuff."

"Like you should talk!" Hakeem snapped in outrage. "I can't believe you snuck out the first night you were punished. I'm tired of covering for you, man."

"Aw, get outta my face. I already covered for you big time with the fight. You didn't take any blame for that, even though you started it." Savon growled, sitting up in his bed.

Hakeem ignored his comment and searched for his notebook, not wanting to leave it with Savon again. His guitar rested exactly where he had put it the previous night, but the notebook was missing. Savon watched him curiously.

"You take my notebook again? I know you already read it once," Hakeem accused, remembering the other night when Savon mentioned Darcy's name.

"No, I didn't take it, but I did look at it. That's 'cause you left it layin' around on the floor where I tripped on it. I was gonna throw it away until I checked and realized it was yours. Maybe I read a little bit too, but you can't tell me you don't look at my stuff when I leave it out."

Hakeem scratched his head, unwilling to get into this fight now. He had to find his journal. The last time he

115

remembered having it was when he was on the couch with Anika. He'd put it down to teach her how to play the guitar, and when she kissed him, he forgot all about it. He felt a sinking feeling in his chest.

She's reading all my stuff, he thought. The book contained all his songs from Bluford, his thoughts about Darcy, and his dad's sickness. It even contained what he wrote about her.

Maybe she didn't read it, he hoped, stopping at Anika's house on the way to work. He knocked loudly several times, knowing that her grandmother had a hearing aid. There was no answer. He decided to check the laundromat.

Rushing in the door, he went straight to the back where she had been the day before. An unfamiliar young woman watched him nervously as he approached.

"Can I help you?"

"Is Anika here?" he asked.

"No, she don't work on Fridays."

Hakeem shook his head in frustration. By the time he'd see her, she'd probably have read his entire book. Still, there was nothing he could do now. He had to get to work.

At the furniture store, the morning

dragged by like a boring movie. Hakeem looked at the clock periodically, thinking that hours had passed, only to discover that less than half the time had gone by. By noon, he had finished all the usual tasks and began looking for extra work, anything to keep his mind off his father's doctor visit.

After lunch, he swept the parking lot outside the store and pulled the scraggly weeds that grew between the cracks in the asphalt.

By late afternoon, when his mother hadn't called, he began to worry. Even Uncle James seemed edgy.

"I know what you're thinking, Hakeem, but don't worry. These medical tests can take all day sometimes," he said. But Hakeem noticed Uncle James checking his watch often. At 4:00 he even sighed out loud.

"Whatever happens, Hakeem, I want you to know we'll take care of you. You always got a home here with us," Uncle James said at 5:15. The comment scared Hakeem more than it calmed him. It sounded final, as if Dad was going to get sick again, or worse.

It wasn't until 6:30, when Hakeem saw the Nissan pulling slowly into the lot, that his stomach trembled and he began to feel sick.

"I'm sorry I'm late," Mom said, as she stepped out the car. "The tests took forever, and then traffic, and by the time I dropped your father off—"

"I don't care, Mom. Tell us what the doctor said," Hakeem asked.

His mother's face beamed, and she flashed a wide smile. "He's okay, baby! He's okay."

"Really?" Hakeem said, almost not believing the news as his mother's arms wrapped around him. Tears rolled down his face.

"Detroit's been good to us," she explained, her own tears mingling with his. "I don't know if it's your aunt's cookin', the extra rest, or just getting away from all the financial stress, but your father also gained four pounds."

"Really?" Hakeem repeated. He had so expected bad news that he didn't know how to respond to anything else.

"The doctor said he's all clear. He can even start light work in a few weeks."

"That's it. The store is closed tonight," Uncle James said. "We're celebrating."

The news was the best thing Hakeem had heard in months, and for once his heart soared free of the burden it had been under for weeks.

Thank you, God, he thought to himself, leaning back in the car seat, the news seeping deeper into his mind like rain water.

As he listened to his mother gush about how happy she was, the worry that had quietly gripped his heart for so long began to let go. In its place, a mix of emotions that he'd buried away began to well and bubble inside him like steam from a quenched fire.

Since Dad's illness, Hakeem had done nothing but work, assist, support, and help. In that same time, he'd lost his school, his home, his friends. Now with Dad okay, he could no longer ignore how alone he had become. And as Hakeem thought of the months ahead, it only seemed like it would get worse.

Stop feeling sorry for yourself. At least Dad's okay, he thought as they drove home through the evening traffic. Yet Hakeem could not shake the tinge of gloom that began to creep into this thoughts, despite the news of his father's victory over cancer.

As Mom parked the car, Hakeem looked over at Anika's house. A light in the second floor bedroom was on. *Anika must be home*, he thought.

Inside, Hakeem went straight to his father to celebrate.

"I heard the good news, Dad. Someone's gaining weight," Hakeem said, patting Dad's stomach playfully.

"It's all that cookin' your aunt's been doing," Dad joked as he hugged Hakeem. "And it's because of your help, son. You're really helping out, and I want you to know it," he said as they embraced.

"Thanks, Dad," Hakeem said, loosely hugging his father. He was grateful, but even in his father's arms, he felt uneasy. Though he hid it, he was not completely happy, not with his heart divided about the move. Not with Savon watching him. Not with the knowledge that he'd start the school year in the fall without friends. Not with Anika leaving.

What's wrong with me? he thought, angry at himself for being unable to fully enjoy the moment with his family.

After dinner, Hakeem headed over to Anika's house. His father's news made the notebook seem less important. But what Hakeem really wanted was to see

Anika. As he stepped up the front stairs, he noticed her house was dark except for the upstairs light. But then something else caught his eye. The front door was slightly ajar.

It just didn't seem right. Hakeem knew Anika wouldn't forget to lock a door. She was smarter than that.

"Anika?" Hakeem spoke out. The house was deathly silent. "Hello?" he said, louder this time. Still no answer.

He gently nudged the door and it opened halfway with a slight squeak. The familiar musty smell leaked into his nostrils. Hakeem looked back at his uncle's house and then the other way. He saw no one nearby on the street. In the distance, a group of kids hung out under the streetlight on the corner, but no one seemed to notice him.

"Anika?" he yelled and stepped inside.

Other than the open door, the outside of the house was the same as before. But in the living room, Hakeem noticed that the picture of Anika's cousin had been removed. He examined the spot where it had been. A tiny nail was still lodged in the wall where it hung. The remaining photos were undisturbed, a line of strangers gazing at the vacant living room.

A tremor raced down Hakeem's spine.

He moved to where he had sat with Anika the night before. He saw the place where he had put down his notebook, but it wasn't there.

Walking over to the bottom of the stairway, he could see dim yellow light coming from upstairs.

What if someone is hurt? he thought. But his suspicion told him otherwise.

"Hello," he said one more time, carefully making his way up the stairs. At the top was a bathroom and a small hallway with two doors. Both were open, but light came from the farther one that overlooked the street. He walked over to it.

His eyes widened at what he knew was Anika's bedroom. A row of shoes lined the floor against the wall, and next to them stood a coat rack that held a jacket and a few purses. Hakeem noticed that several pairs of shoes had been removed from the row, and not every peg on the rack was holding something. The bed was covered in flowery sheets, but it was unmade. Next to the bed was a tiny plastic alarm clock with red digital numbers.

But what caught Hakeem's eye most was a bus schedule. It sat next to the clock, underneath the light that had been left on. Picking it up, he noticed that several times had been circled. All of them left the bus terminal between 10:00 p.m. and 2:00 a.m.

"She's gone," Hakeem said in shock.

He walked back to the second bedroom and flipped the nearest light switch. The room was clean and sparse. Old pictures were arranged neatly on the walls, but several had been removed. Two drawers were open and empty as if they had been quickly packed. The bed itself was unmade, but a pile of folded laundry had been positioned on a nightstand. A note written in large letters was left on top of the pile.

I love you, Grandma. Sorry I had to leave. The nurse will be here this afternoon to take you to the care center. Your bags are packed downstairs. I put Grandpa's picture in the bag for you. I know you'll be in good hands. Thank you for understanding. I will call you when I can. Don't worry about me.

Love, Anika

Hakeem noticed two tiny circles on the bottom corner of paper, as if teardrops had landed on there. His hands shook as he put the letter back, his own eyes moist.

Looking at the room, Hakeem knew what Anika said the other day was true. The state people had come for her grandmother, and she had run away to avoid foster care. He hated her decision, but he couldn't help but admire her. Alone in an impossible situation, she did the best she could for her grandmother, staying as long as possible without anyone to help her. And when she knew there was nothing more that she could do, she took a bold step and went where she wanted to be. It was a decision he envied even as he dismissed it as a fantasy the night before.

"I'll miss you, girl," he said aloud as he descended the stairs. Once outside, he carefully closed and locked the door behind him, treating the empty house as if it were the grave of a loved one.

Hakeem went straight upstairs as soon as he got back to Uncle Jason's. His family, including Savon, was in the living room eating ice cream and watching TV. On the screen, a police car raced through a crowded city street in pursuit of a criminal.

Upstairs, he grabbed his guitar and cried through its strings, the sharp pain gradually giving way to a dull ache. His thoughts drifted to the friend he lost next door and the others he left back home. His only comfort was his guitar, but even that reminded him of Anika.

She was gone, and with her, all his songs, his words, his memories. Part of his soul. She did take things, as Uncle James and Savon warned, but for some reason he couldn't be mad at her.

Putting the guitar down, Hakeem stretched out on his bed and imagined what it would have been like to take the bus with her back to California. He pictured being dropped off at Bluford, a place that seemed farther away each passing day. He tried to envision his friends and how they would welcome him, but instead all they did was wave goodbye. And as his tired eyes closed, Hakeem resigned himself to a simple undeniable fact: he had never felt more alone.

Chapter 9

The night faded into a blur until Hakeem heard a thud and glanced up at his clock. It was 12:15. Immediately, he felt as if his stomach sank through his mattress onto the floor.

Savon. It was Friday night. He had to know for sure about Savon.

Hakeem bolted upright in his bed. The room was dark except for the night-light. But even in its dim glow, he could see that Savon was gone. Hakeem cursed himself for falling asleep.

But then, just above a whisper, he heard it. A thin metallic squeak. Then a soft thud.

Hakeem peered out the open window. Someone was walking away from the house. It had to be his cousin.

Scrambling out the window, Hakeem

nearly rolled off the roof, a drop that would certainly break bones. Unused to the roof, he fumbled at the iron railing before finally getting a good grip. The iron protested his weight with a slight groan, but it held him, and he carefully climbed to the ground, his hands moist from dew that covered the metal.

On the street, a dog barked somewhere in the distance. Hakeem heard a truck pass on the block behind Uncle James's house. But his street was quiet. Savon was on a far corner heading toward the avenue that led to his father's furniture store. He was heading straight to the area where all the robberies occurred. Hakeem rushed to get closer but had to wait at a cross street as a dark SUV drove past, its stereo rumbling like a rolling earthquake.

Hakeem wondered what he would do if it turned out Savon was a thief. He didn't know if he could snitch on his own cousin. Telling Uncle James was one thing; telling the police was something else. He hoped Savon wasn't going to put him in a position where he'd have to decide. But as he trailed his cousin closer and closer to the trouble spot, he grew more certain that his worst fears about Savon were true.

Just as Hakeem had cut the distance between himself and his cousin in half, Savon darted into a side street lined with cars and then squeezed through a broken fence that surrounded a parking lot. Hakeem began to get scared. Once he took the turn into the lot, he was disoriented. He wasn't sure if he could find his way home alone, and yet no one knew where he was. Even if he saw a police officer, what could he say?

Excuse me officer, I am trying to make sure my cousin doesn't rob a store, he thought angrily. That wouldn't work, unless he wanted to get in trouble for being out after curfew.

Hakeem knew he had to stay close to Savon. Now it was a matter of survival. Focusing on the crowded lot, Hakeem spotted his cousin snaking between the cars ahead of him. The distance between them was about the length of a basketball court. Hakeem knew they couldn't be too far from his uncle's store, but he couldn't see it. Somehow, Savon had led him to an alley that went behind all the businesses on the main avenue. All he could see was the backs of warehouses, loading docks, dumpsters, and parking lots.

128

But as he neared the halfway point of the lot, he heard music.

Another car with a loud system, he thought.

Up ahead, on the far side of the lot, Savon stopped suddenly and looked around. Four guys rounded the corner and joined him.

"You ready to do this?" one of them said. Hakeem stopped. He recognized the voice. It was Tariq.

"You know it," Savon barked. The guys crossed the street fast.

Hakeem couldn't believe his eyes. His cousin and his friends were going to rob someone's business. Right now. They were ready to break in through the back of a building just as they had done at Mr. Sung's store. Hakeem had to do something. He looked for a pay phone to call home. None was in sight.

Running to stay close, he raced to the edge of the lot. There was a phone on the corner a block ahead. Hakeem was about to sprint toward it when Savon and his friends surrounded a dark doorway at the rear of a brick building. Music drowned whatever words were being said, but to Hakeem's surprise the door opened, and the group moved inside. An overhead light illuminated each person's face as they passed. Savon was first in line. As Hakeem watched, a second group of people approached the door and went in.

Hakeem crossed the street and moved toward the door. The music grew steadily louder as he approached. It came from inside the building, not the street, he realized, feeling the air vibrate with sound. He rushed to the spot where Savon and his friends stood.

To his surprise, the door creaked open, and an enormous man with a shaved head and thick arms emerged.

"I don't know you," he said, examining Hakeem as if he had committed a crime. "You got to go 'round the front." The man pointed opposite the direction of the parking lot. Hakeem tried to peer around the man, but he couldn't see anything inside.

"What is this place?" Hakeem asked.

The man suddenly looked insulted. "If you don't know that, you shouldn't be here," he grumbled. The door closed in Hakeem's face.

Hakeem rounded the corner and came face to face with a crowd of young people gathered in front a set of double doors. A sign above them read "The Street," and just beneath were the words:

Friday Night
18 and Under
Live and Local Hip Hop

It was a club, Hakeem realized. He had gone to one with Darcy on their first date last year. But why was Savon sneaking to a club in the middle of the night? Hakeem shook his head in confusion. It didn't make any sense. Why the secrecy?

"Yo, watch your step!" someone growled, snapping Hakeem out of his thoughts and pushing him forward.

Following the throng of people, he stepped through a metal detector, got frisked by a security guard, paid a five dollar "door charge," and emerged into a world unlike anything he'd seen back home.

Amidst a pulsing hip hop beat that cracked and ground the air, people were moving and swaying in rhythm. Others, standing to the side, bobbed their heads to the music and watched people passing. The floor sloped downward to a small stage illuminated by spotlights hanging in the ceiling. On the stage, two rappers performed. Their performance charged the crowd, which raised its arms and cheered in approval. Hakeem searched for his cousin as a new beat mixed in. What he saw next made his jaw drop in surprise.

Savon and his friends burst onto the stage as if they had been shot from a cannon. Hakeem gaped as his cousin strutted with poise and skill to the beat. Arms everywhere waved, heads swayed, and Savon delivered his words like sermons of power.

> Step back! Here comes the
> outcast,
> Makin' you move wit' da spells dat
> my rhymes cast
>
> Pushin' and pulling you,
> my words subliminal
> I got mad skills, but I ain't a criminal
>
> Others judge and try to hate me
> But when they hear my beats, they
> can't escape me
>
> 'Cause I'm a lyrical deliverer, the
> rhythmical superior
> Always misunderstood, but never
> inferior . . .

Hakeem stood dumbfounded, his mind spinning like a whirlwind. Savon's behavior over the last week suddenly made sense. The late hours, the mysterious plans, the desperate need to be out Friday night. None of it had anything to do with robbery. His cousin was a rapper, not a thief. Hakeem felt a wave of relief and regret for what he had thought all along.

On the stage, Savon had charisma, commanding attention with each step he took. And as he strutted across the stage, he seemed driven by his music.

Watching him, Hakeem understood exactly what Savon was feeling. It was the same as when he played his guitar. Like him, Savon used writing and music to respond to the world around him, to vent his frustration, to react. In many ways, he realized, they weren't that different. Raising his arms upward, Hakeem joined the crowd in support of his cousin.

"*Blood is thicker*," Uncle James had said. For the first time, those words seemed true.

But there were still so many unanswered questions.

Savon and his crew performed several

songs and then left the stage in a chorus of cheers. As soon as they finished, three guys immediately took their place and began a performance of their own. The crowd swayed and moved for the new performers, and Hakeem began to search for Savon. He had to talk to him. At the very least, he owed his cousin an apology.

Darting through the shadows, the blinding stage lights, and the throng of moving bodies, Hakeem checked each area of the club, but he couldn't find Savon. Near the main stage, a teenager bumped into him and offered to sell him drugs. "I got what you need, man," the kid said.

"I'm cool," Hakeem replied, stepping away. Similar things had happened at Bluford. But here, alone in an unfamiliar place, he didn't feel as safe. He looked at the clock. It was already past 2:30 a.m., and he still had the unfamiliar walk home. Then he had to climb back in the bedroom window and try not to wake his family. Lost in a sea of strangers, Hakeem began to worry. He decided to check the men's restroom. If Savon wasn't there, he'd try to walk back alone.

The bathroom was crowded when he

stepped in, but Hakeem noticed that everyone in there was standing around talking. In the far corner, three guys were huddled together; one was counting money. The tallest of the three nodded at Hakeem.

"Whatcha lookin' for, man?" he asked. "Maybe I can help you find it." Several guys in the bathroom laughed. Hakeem's instinct told him to leave.

"My cousin," Hakeem replied, turning away.

"Ain't no cousin of yours in here. I ain't ever seen you before. Where you from?"

Hakeem turned to leave and bumped into the kid who tried to sell him drugs outside. "Yo, watch your step!" the kid said.

Hakeem tried to go around him, but the kid moved to block his path.

"What you runnin' from, man?" came the first voice. Before he could move, Hakeem felt someone grab him from behind, tugging him away from the door. Several hands began checking his pockets for money. "You got anything for us?"

"Get off me," Hakeem commanded, twisting unsuccessfully against them. Within seconds, he was completely surrounded. He knew something bad was about to happen, but he was powerless to stop it.

Then, like an explosion, a familiar voiced boomed. "Let him go!"

Hakeem turned back to see Savon, Tariq, and their friends.

"That's my blood, yo! That's my cousin. Let him go!"

Hakeem felt the grip on him loosen immediately.

"Why didn't you say you was *Savon's* cousin?" one kid said, looking at Hakeem in disgust.

"C'mon, cuz, we gotta bounce," Savon said, pulling Hakeem away from the circle of young men. In an instant, Hakeem was outside with Savon and his friends. He felt embarrassed as he looked at their serious faces and struggled to shake off the attack.

"I gotta get this boy home before he gets me in more trouble," Savon explained. Then he shook hands with the members of his crew. Seconds later he turned to Hakeem. "Let's go," he said firmly.

Together they crossed the parking lot in dark silence as if neither knew how to talk about what just happened.

Hakeem had much to say, but he didn't know where to begin. He was grateful for his cousin's help and impressed with his performance. And more than anything, he was relieved that Savon was not the thief he imagined. Yet he was also angry. Had Savon treated him differently, just told him the truth, he would not have snuck around in the dark. He would not have been forced to lie to his father. He would not have ended up trapped in a bathroom by a gang. As they walked, Hakeem's anger nearly held back the apology he knew he owed his cousin.

"What were you thinkin'?" Savon asked finally, breaking this silence. "If Tariq didn't see you go into that bathroom, you'd a got a beat-down. Everybody knows not to go in that bathroom after midnight. It's dangerous," he said.

"I was lookin' for *you*," Hakeem replied.

"*Why*? So you could lecture me like Dad about how I was throwin' my life away, doin' somethin' stupid, hangin' wit' the wrong crowd," he said, shaking his head. "I ain't havin' that."

"No, Savon," Hakeem said, swallowing his pride. "I was tryin' to find you to apologize 'cause I had you all wrong. You were good up there tonight, the best rapper on that the stage."

Savon's eyes widened at Hakeem's comment, as if kind words from someone in his family were not what he expected. For several minutes they crossed the quiet streets without a word, but then Savon kicked a can along the curb, and turned to Hakeem.

"Know what my pops did when I told him I make money rapping at clubs and house parties? He told me I needed to get a real job before I ended up in jail. Since you showed up, he only got worse. Now he don't say nothin' to me except how good you are and what a *disappointment* I am," Savon said bitterly.

"I'm sorry, Savon," Hakeem said, beginning to understand his cousin's frustration. In his attempt to guide Savon, Uncle James was treating him unfairly and pushing him away. If it weren't for his friends, Hakeem realized, Savon would be completely alone too.

"You ever try to talk to him?" Hakeem asked.

"*Talk*," Savon scoffed. "He don't listen to me. All he cares about is work."

Again, Hakeem heard the pain in

Savon's voice, and he knew there was some truth in his words. But he also knew it wasn't easy to talk to Savon. And he had seen Uncle James's deep concern for his son, though Savon couldn't see it.

I was just hoping you could talk some sense into him, Uncle James had said days ago.

"You two need to talk. I mean *really* talk," Hakeem suggested.

"You don't understand, cuz. I tried talkin' to him months ago. I told him that me and the boys had been re-hearsin' and stuff. I even asked him if he wanted to see us perform, but all he could talk about was the store, and how he needed me there all the time.

"I was like 'But Dad, I been workin' here since I was twelve years old. Can't I do my own thing for once just on week-ends?' He told me no, that I was goin' to be wastin' my time or somethin'. He don't even know what I do, and he starts actin' like I'm becomin' a criminal. You know what it's like to have your own father disrespect you like that?" Savon asked, his voice wavering slightly.

"I know you don't 'cause your dad believes in you," Savon answered his own question. "The way I see it, if my dad can't support me, why am I goin' to spend the rest of my life doin' what *he* says? Besides, he don't need me anyway. He's got you," Savon said as they turned a corner.

"The day you and I fought, he said he was ready to kick me out. I'm done with him, and he's done with me," he added bitterly.

For an instant, Hakeem almost thought he saw Savon's eyes water, but he said nothing, letting his cousin recover. As they neared the house, Savon stopped suddenly, his eyes wide open.

"Oh, no," he said heavily.

Hakeem followed Savon's gaze toward the house. All the lights on the first and second floor were on. That could mean only one thing. Someone had discovered they were out.

"We're busted," Savon added. "Dad's gonna kick me out."

"No he's not," Hakeem assured him, imagining the look on his own father's face when he discovered his empty bed. He could almost feel Mom worrying about him as he neared the house. "We'll talk to them together."

"Don't you get it, cuz? I can't sit

through Dad rippin' me. Not again," Savon said. He looked defeated. The fearless stage performer was now suddenly human, a boy fearing the wrath of his father. "I can't do it."

Hakeem stood next to him. "Savon, you're not in this alone. I got your back. We'll talk to them together as a family. I'm serious. C'mon," he urged.

Savon looked at him, took a deep breath, and then stared at the front door.

"You go first," he said.

Chapter 10

"There they are!" Aunt Lorraine cried, as Hakeem and Savon walked in the door. "We were worried sick about you."

"Are you okay?" Mom asked, rushing over to Hakeem.

"We're fine," Hakeem said, gently shrugging away from her.

Uncle James tore into the room and glared at his son. "Bein' a screw-up wasn't enough? Now you gonna drag your cousin into your mess too?"

"But Dad—"

"Shut your mouth, boy," Uncle James yelled. "I told you last time that I wasn't playin', and you pushed me. You wanna ignore my rules, then you can get outta my house. Maybe then you'll learn something. You best start packin'," he commanded.

Hakeem watched in anger as Savon's fears became true.

"Easy, James," Dad said.

"I'm sorry, but this doesn't concern you. This is between me and my son."

Dad took a step back. The air in the small living room suddenly grew charged like the instant before a lightning strike.

"You see, Hakeem," Savon said, tears in his eyes as he walked toward the stairs. "He don't listen to me."

"Wait, Savon," Hakeem urged, the silence he held for so many months beginning to crack. Everyone in the room turned to him.

"Hakeem, you don't have to cover for him," Mom said, looking at the bruise Hakeem still had on his face from his fight with Savon.

"I'm not covering for him!" Hakeem said, struggling to contain the fury in his chest. "All of you listen to me. You got us all wrong. Savon practically saved my life tonight."

"*What*?" Uncle James asked. Mom turned in surprise.

"What are you sayin', Hakeem?" Dad said.

"All of you been acting like Savon's a

143

criminal, and I'm this p-p-perfect person. That's not fair and it's not true!" Hakeem yelled, his hands shaking with emotion.

Everyone gaped as Hakeem recounted the entire week, including his early fears about Savon, the details he hid from his father, and the dramatic events he experienced at the club. All the adults except James reacted in surprise, especially when Hakeem told them about Savon's performance and the incident in the bathroom.

Hakeem even mentioned the conversation he and Savon had outside and how much Savon doubted Uncle James would listen to him.

"I didn't tell you the whole truth this week because I wasn't sure what it was, but I'm sure now," Hakeem concluded. "The truth is that Savon isn't doing anything illegal. And if you saw him tonight, you wouldn't be disappointed in him, Uncle James. You'd be proud."

"Hakeem, I appreciate what you are trying to do here, but I don't need your advice about how I should raise my son. When you're a parent, you'll understand how hard it is to bring up a child and how you gotta make tough decisions.

144

Savon chose to leave the store and dis-obey me, and he's got to face the conse-quences of his actions," Uncle James said sternly.

"But Uncle James—"

"Enough, Hakeem! Stay out of it," Uncle James barked.

"Easy, James," Hakeem's father warned.

"Why you gotta be like that, Dad?" Savon demanded, glaring at Uncle James. "Hakeem's tellin' you the truth, and you still don't want to listen."

"No, *you* are the one that didn't lis-ten. I told you the other day this was your last chance. I don't want to send you out, but you made a choice, and part of being a man is you gotta live with that choice. Go up and pack your bags," James ordered.

Savon blinked, shook his head, and walked to the stairway. Hakeem felt as if he was watching two massive trains rac-ing into each other, and he was power-less to stop them. His uncle and cousin were completely out of control.

"Everyone just stop!" a voice yelled suddenly. Hakeem turned to see Aunt Lorraine step into the center of the living room. "All y'all are acting like the kids I teach at school, and I can't stand it no more. I always knew the men in this family were stubborn, but this is ridiculous," she said, putting her hands on her hips.

Uncle James looked surprised, and Savon stopped in his tracks.

"Nobody's going anyhere until we figure this out. James, you think Savon's gonna be any safer if we kick him out now?" she said, quickly turning to Savon. "And do you think sneakin' out in the dark and leavin' your father all alone at the store every day is the way to get him to listen to you?"

Savon shrugged. "I didn't want to leave him all alone, Mom. I told him I could still work in the store part time, but that I needed time for me and the boys. Tariq's workin' at the music store, and he got us some gigs at parties this summer. I already saved $300. I told Dad we were makin' money, but he didn't want to hear it. All he wants to hear about is the store," Savon said wearily.

"Savon, that ain't true," Uncle James replied. "Yes, I could use your help, but that's besides the point. I know two families from church who got boys your age in jail. I know another who lost her son 'cause he was shot outside a club by mistake. I'm not gonna let that happen to you. And if I gotta be tough, that's what I'm gonna do. It ain't 'cause I don't care. It's because I *do* care."

"Yeah, well you sure got a strange way of showing it," Savon grumbled.

"And so do you," Aunt Lorraine countered. "You been given us attitude for months now. That hasn't helped anything."

"That's cause all you do is tell me I should be more like Hakeem. It's like you want him around more than me or somethin'. The more you do that, the more I feel like just givin' up, you know, 'cause I'm never gonna be like him, the A student, the perfect son," Savon replied, his voice a mixture of sadness and resentment.

"There's no one we love around here more than you, Savon. It's just we thought you'd listen to Hakeem since you wouldn't listen to us," Aunt Lorraine explained. "You two used to be so close."

Hakeem winced at the mention of his name. He hated how Savon and his parents threw it around at each other like an insult.

"Can you all just leave me out of

this?" Hakeem cut in, unable to hide his own resentment. "I'm *not* perfect. Ever since I got here, all of you have thrown me in the middle of your fight, and I been getting nothing but static from all sides," Hakeem confessed, forcing back the emotions that formed a huge lump in his throat. "All I know is it ain't easy being out here away from home. But you all keep saying I got my act together. I don't know where you get that. Right now, I am just tryin' to survive out here, that's all. The more you all say I am perfect, the more I want to go home to the people that know me 'cause none of them would treat me like this."

Hakeem's parents looked surprised at his words. They glanced over at Aunt Lorraine and Uncle James, who just shook their heads as if they were stunned. Savon nodded thoughtfully.

"Looks like there's lots of misunderstanding in this family from all of us," Dad said, rubbing his eyes. It was past 3:00 a.m.

"Yeah, but there's lots of love too," Mom added, and the adults in the room nodded.

Just then Charmaine and Charlene walked into the living room, their eyes squinting against the bright lights.

"Why is everyone up so late?" Charmaine asked.

"We can't sleep 'cause everyone keeps talking," protested Charlene.

"Girls, go back to bed. All of us are going to bed now," Mom said, leading them to their bedroom.

"Amen. Let's sleep on this. We got lots to talk about, but we're not going to solve it all tonight," Uncle James said.

"Do I still gotta leave?" Savon asked.

"No, son, I don't want that. I never did. But if you stay, you're gonna have to make some changes around here," Uncle James said, looking at Aunt Lorraine, who stared at him. "Maybe I do too, but let's talk about it tomorrow."

Savon sighed as if he had been released from a great burden. "Thanks, pop," he said, heading upstairs. Hakeem followed him, exhausted by the day's events.

"Cuz, wake up. You got a phone call. I think it's important."

Hakeem was about to roll over and go back to sleep. But Savon's voice was sincere. The hostile edge that had been in it all week was gone.

Hakeem sat up, rubbed his eyes, and made his way downstairs.

His parents sat at the table, the looks on their faces grave.

"Hello?"

"Hakeem, it's me." The voice snapped him to attention. It was Tarah, but she sounded more stressed than he'd ever heard her. She was calling from California. "I can't stay on the phone long, and I got bad news to tell you. Darcy's grandmother died last night."

Hakeem groaned and leaned his head against the wall, his mind flooded with memories of the nice old woman he'd seen each time he visited Darcy. He could almost feel Darcy's loss across the thousands of miles that separated them. If he hadn't moved, he'd be with her this very moment.

"Darcy's in real bad shape," Tarah continued. "She needs you."

"I'll be there. I'll figure out a way."

"I knew you would, Hakeem," she said.

After he hung up the phone, he explained the situation to his parents.

"Hakeem, I know it's important to you, but we don't have that kind of money right now, and we can't ask your aunt and uncle. They've already done too much."

"I got money," a voice said from behind them. It was Savon. He was standing at the bottom of the steps holding his bundle of cash. Everyone turned to him at once in shock.

"I've been savin' what I make at parties so me and my boys can make a demo CD, but if you can pay me back this summer, you can borrow it."

"I'll work all summer to pay it back if I have to," Hakeem insisted.

"Are you sure about this, Savon?" Dad asked. "That's a lot of money."

"Yeah, I'm sure," he insisted. "He stuck his neck out for me. It's only right that I pay him back."

"Thanks, Savon," Hakeem said, grateful for his cousin and the difficult path that finally reconnected them. "I owe you one."

In one week, a lifetime can pass
In one day, families shatter like glass
In one hour, time still moves too fast
In one second, we make choices that
*   last.*

Hakeem wrote the words in a new notebook as his airplane touched down.

It was the same airport he'd left days ago. But the person who walked through then was not the same one who passed through now. Hakeem had gone through a fire and been transformed.

As he stepped from the taxi in front of Holy Redeemer Church, Hakeem didn't know what he would say to Darcy. But he knew that he belonged at her side with his friends.

He spotted Darcy as soon as he entered the church. She was standing before the congregation delivering a powerful tribute to her grandmother, who rested in an open coffin before her. Watching her struggle against tears, Hakeem missed Darcy more than ever.

He noticed Cooper and Tarah nearby, but at the conclusion of the service, he headed straight to Darcy, whose eyes poured tears when she spotted him.

"Hakeem! I can't believe you're here!" Darcy exclaimed, throwing her arms around him the way she did when they parted. "How—"

"Tarah called and told me what happened, and I wanted to be here for you, Darcy," Hakeem explained, feeling himself drawn to the warmth of her face and the hurt in her eyes. She looked older somehow, as if the ten days apart had transformed her as much as they had transformed him. Despite the changes, Hakeem knew one thing was certain: he loved her like no other.

"You look different," Hakeem said as they left the church together.

"I *am* different," Darcy replied, her words passionate and mysterious.

Me too, Darcy, Hakeem thought as he walked hand-in-hand with her back to the neighborhood he had known all his life.

Gazing at the familiar people that had silently gathered around them in support, Hakeem felt a powerful and unrelenting voice stir in his soul.

This is where I belong, the voice said. *This is my home.*

When Hakeem arrived back in Detroit two days later, a strange package sat on his bed.

"That was in the mailbox for you," Savon said on his way out. "I'm goin' to the store to help Dad. While you were gone, we made a deal. I work in the store three days a week. He comes to see me and the boys rap at this block party on July 4th. I still can't believe he's gonna show up, but I heard him say it."

"Cool!" Hakeem exclaimed. "Maybe I'll play my guitar too."

"Let's not get crazy, cuz," Savon said with a playful smirk. "Oh, one other thing. The cops finally busted them thieves the other night. I'm still gonna try and convince Dad to get that rottie. Later," he said.

Hakeem examined the package. It had no return address. He shook it several times and then tore it open. Inside was his notebook, a bit more tattered than when he'd last seen it. He leafed through the pages and saw that everything was intact. But on the last page, there was a note he'd never seen before.

Dear Hakeem,

By the time you read this, I will be long gone. The state people took Grandma like I told you they would. I just couldn't go to a foster home, not even for six months. I hope you understand.

Before you got here, I was mixed up in some things with Rasul and his crew. It's why Savon and I broke up two years ago. Rasul's been causing trouble for a while now, mostly breaking into stores around the way. I even helped his crew a few times, holding money for them. I know it was stupid, and I'm not proud of what I did, but I've been trying to get out of that for a long time. Then you came along, and when Rasul started making plans to hit your uncle's store, I had to end it.

When I called the police and told them everything, I knew I was making things right, but I got scared too. If he found out who turned him in, Rasul would do everything he could to make me sorry. Another reason to run.

I meant what I said to you the other day. I wish I met you sooner. Don't forget our kiss. I won't. Where I am going isn't far from Bluford High School. If you ever come back, maybe I'll see you again. My phone number is on the back of the page you wrote about me. Call me some-time.

Love,
Anika

P.S.—Throw away this note.

Hakeem read the letter several times before shredding it into tiny scraps. But by then, all of Anika's words were etched in his memory, and he had the funny feeling that he might see her again one day.